GOOD-BYE
MY WISHING
STAR

Look for these and other Apple Paperbacks
in your local bookstore!

The Gift Horse
by Sheila Hayes

You Shouldn't Have To Say Good-bye
by Patricia Hermes

New Girl
by Stella Pevsner

Amy Moves In
by Marilyn Sachs

Summer Stories
by Nola Thacker

GOOD-BYE MY WISHING STAR

Vicki Grove

AN
APPLE
PAPERBACK

SCHOLASTIC INC.
New York Toronto London Auckland Sydney

ISBN 0-590-42152-2

12 11 10 9 8 7 6 5 4   1 2 3 4/9

Printed in the U.S.A.   28

First Scholastic printing, July 1989

To my family

Contents

GOOD-BYE
MY WISHING
STAR

1 *To Whoever Finds This*

If these pages are covered with dirt and wasps' nests and stuff, I'm sorry. I'm writing in the hayloft so Roger can't find me and get his sticky hands all over everything. I'll leave this here when I'm done, hidden under the hay, and if you find it and read it you'll know what the last weeks have been like for us.

I'm Jens. Jens Tucker. I'm twelve years old and this was my farm before it was yours. At least I imagine you're the one who bought it, if you found this. You may wonder why I'm wasting the perfectly new, beautiful red diary that Shelley just gave me for the purpose of writing about a whole bunch of sad stuff.

Well, mostly because it will give me something to do for the next two weeks until we move. Right now there's always a lump in my throat and Mama keeps accusing me of moping, which I'm not, but anyway . . .

Also, I can't just leave without finishing things up, and writing about this whole thing just somehow seems to finish it. Does that make any sense to you?

I think I'm leaving this for you instead of taking it with me because I figure it may make you really appreciate what you've got here, if you know how much I'm somewhere missing it. I figure leaving will be an ache in me for a long, long time. Maybe forever.

I know I don't have time in two weeks or room in this diary to write about all the years I spent growing up here. Everywhere I look there's just so much to say good-bye to.

So I guess I'll start with about ten weeks ago, because the first inkling I had that anything was wrong came the day Brenda Miller's father died.

2 *Brenda Miller's Father*

Brenda Miller's father died one late-April afternoon, while we were copying our multiplication problems. There were twenty of them, which wouldn't normally have been that big a deal, but the windows were open and the sun coming through them made it hard to concentrate. I kept thinking about what I was going to do outside when I got home and I could tell everybody else was doing that too. Then Henry yawned real loud, and the rest of us giggled, and Miss Horton frowned and said to get to work or we'd be there all afternoon.

Most of us had all the problems copied when the bell rang. Our principal, Mr. Thompson, was standing in the hall right outside our door, so we had to stay in line and walk till we got past him. I thought he was waiting there to talk to Miss Horton, but he took Brenda aside and led her to his office with his hand on her shoulder. When he was gone we could run and talk, finally.

"Well, John Frank stole my banana again," I told Marla, furiously. He did that every day after lunch, when we were all outside waiting for the bell. He would walk right over, mean as anything, and say, "Well, let's have it." If I hadn't given him one from my lunchbox, it was hard telling what would have happened. Luckily, I didn't like bananas anyway, but still, it was the principle of the thing.

"That's horrible. Just horrible," Marla said, sympathetically.

Marla and I went straight to find a seat together on the bus. She wanted to sit close to Arthur Boatright, but he was sitting beside John Frank. I told her I was very sorry, but John Frank just made me sick to my stomach. She said it didn't matter to her; the only reason she wanted to sit near Arthur was to ask him if his mama had any extra eggs for sale. Her mother had told her to be sure and ask him.

So I sat down by the window, two seats in front of John and Arthur, and Marla sat beside me. Just as the bus started up, I saw Brenda Miller coming out the door of the school into the sunlight. Miss Horton was on one side of her and Mr. Thompson carried her books. The three of them were walking slowly to Mr. Thompson's car.

"What'd Brenda do?" I asked Marla, who was craning around my shoulder to see too.

"Search me. She's not the type to get in trouble."

"No, but it looks like she did anyway," I said, putting a hand over my eyes to see through the window glare. "Looks like she's crying, don't you think?"

Just then somebody threw a paper wad at me and I had to turn around. I turned back to the window as soon as I could and caught a glimpse of Brenda and Miss Horton and Mr. Thompson just as we turned the corner. They looked like three tiny wooden dolls now, as the spring wind whipped the trees around far above their heads.

Mama wasn't very sympathetic about John Frank, as usual.

"I just can't understand, Jens, why you take a banana in the first place, since you don't like them," she said, like she did every day. She went on folding Roger's diapers carefully as if they were made of solid gold or something.

How could I answer her? Sometimes it seems like Mama and I are from different planets.

I just stomped upstairs and changed into older jeans, then went outside to check on my rabbit.

He was in a cage I'd made for him from a bicycle basket turned upside down. It was as solid and tight as a real one. I couldn't see that the rabbit was any bigger than he had been eight hours before. My father had found him for me when he was mowing in the alfalfa field. I could keep him as long as I fed him, made sure he had enough water, and he stayed small. When he grew up he might die if I kept him, so I would have to let him go. But it takes ages and ages for rabbits to get big. So I could really think that he was my own forever and forever. I gave him a lettuce leaf and then decided to go to the field and find him a treat for dessert.

The early clover was all in bloom and the smell blew everywhere. It filled me up so that I had to run and jump in the air, like I had when I was a little kid. Who cared? Nobody was out here in the clover field to see. I whirled in the green and purple field, the wind catching my long brown hair and floating it around me, making me look pretty good for a change. I wondered if a prince was watching from the clouds. Well, of course, one wasn't. But still, anything was possible. That's what Marla always says.

"Anything's possible," she said when Miss Horton came in with a funny ring on her finger that we thought was new. And it turned out that she really was engaged, so see? Marla's saying is true.

Anything is possible, especially, in my opinion, in

an early spring clover field. I fell on my back and watched the clouds and the tall clover leaves blow and dance around me. Someday, ages and ages away, I thought I would remember exactly how these clouds had looked. Or maybe I would just stay here forever, eating clover blossoms and sucking weeds to stay alive.

When I finally sat back up it was getting a little chilly. Mama was standing in the doorway of the kitchen, far in the distance, yelling something against the wind. I went toward her at a run. She said to hurry and gather the eggs and set the table because this was her night for church choir in Iola, and she had to get ready.

It was at choir practice that night that Mama heard the news about Brenda Miller's father, and she told me when she came home.

"Jens, do you know what a heart attack is?" she asked in a quiet voice, looking me in the eyes in a funny kind of way, the kind of way she usually looked at Roger.

"Sure," I said. "I know all about that stuff."

"Well, I just want you to remember that it probably happened very quickly, and he didn't suffer," she said. "These things just happen sometimes."

"Sure, Mama, I know. I'm not a baby."

I went up to my room then to work on my multiplication problems but sat instead, staring out my window at the star outline around the milk shed, wondering what a heart attack was. Brenda had been looking at these very problems, had been copying these very numbers when it happened. She looked like her father. I had seen him once. His hair was black, like hers. She had his very hair on her, falling in her eyes as she bent to copy her problems. One second there he was, and then wasn't, as she worked away and didn't know it. As the sunlight danced on the blackboard, beneath the trees, beneath the clouds . . . as the wind raced over the clover.

I slammed my notebook shut and grabbed my jacket, but out in the hall my parents' voices, below me in the kitchen, stopped me on the stairs.

"They can call it whatever they want, it's the day in, day out strain of it all that got Sid." That was my father's voice, slow and quiet.

"Jane Logan said that Sally told her the bank had already foreclosed on them. Sid was driving up to Kansas City every week, putting in his application everywhere he could find. He and Sally were the fourth generation of Millers on that farm. It's no wonder it broke Sid's heart to lose it." My mother's gentle voice had gotten quieter as she talked, and had a tremble in it.

And then everything was real quiet for a few seconds, and I heard my father clear his throat a few times. He does that when the tractor needs something that costs a lot, or when there's too much rain in September and he can't get into the fields to harvest the soybeans. He just sits by the window then, staring and clearing his throat, and Mama and I go quietly around him.

"There's not a farmer hereabouts it couldn't happen to," he said, finally. "This land will eat us all alive before it's through."

I'd never heard him talk like that, say such scary things in a voice that low and hollow. I ran then, down the stairs and through the front room. I let the screen door bang behind me. I was too upset to wait to close it gently, though I knew they might be mad if they knew I'd been listening to them. I had to smell the clover, had to hear the gentle wind, feel the warmth of the earth.

When I was far in the field I fell on my back. But the ground was damp now, the moon looked old. I ran home again, faster than I can ever remember running.

When I was safe in bed I asked Mama if I could sleep with the hall light on, and she let me.

Brenda wasn't at school the next day or the next. We all figured she would be back Monday.

"Why don't we get Brenda something with our club money?" I suggested to Shelley when we were hanging around at first recess. The idea just floated into my mind from somewhere.

Marla and a couple of other girls and I had a club that we'd started the summer before when it was hot and July and we needed something to do. We didn't really meet any more, since we were in sixth grade now and it might look stupid, but we had all paid dues of twenty-five cents when we started, and that money was still sitting around in Marla's duck bank on her dresser.

"Yeah!" she agreed immediately. Shelley is what you'd call perky. She jumped up and down now, her short black curls bobbing, getting into the spirit of the thing. "We can all go out Saturday to Iola to do the shopping around! My mom will drive us."

And so, we did. Marla and Shelley sat in the front seat with Shelley's mom for the ten-minute drive into town from Shelley's farm, where we had all met. Kate and I sat in back, fishing the quarters out of Marla's duck bank with a butter knife.

It's not hard to shop in Iola. There's only one store. There are also two elevators, a United States post office, a Methodist church, a gas station, and a pink brick building that used to be a bank but is now occupied by Jack Shire's collection of six Oldsmobile convertibles, none of which run. Just a couple of blocks outside of town is our red brick school building.

"I don't mind taking you girls clear in to Crestville if you can't find anything here," Shelley's mom told us as she let us out beside Hempen's General Store and Video Rental Shoppe.

"That's okay, Mrs. Conover," Marla said, smiling politely. I guess you'd say Marla is the one of the four of us with the best manners. "I'm sure we can find the perfect thing right here at Hempen's."

Personally, I had my doubts. But who was I to butt in? I was only the person who had had the idea in the first place, that was all. The more I thought about that, the more it irked me.

"You could at least have asked the rest of us what we thought, you know," I finally told her. Mrs. Conover had moved the station wagon on down to the elevator, and we could see one of the men there loading feed sacks into the open back. "She's probably going to have the car so loaded up now that she won't want to drive that far if we change our minds."

Marla looked hurt and opened her mouth to say something. But Shelley was standing at Hempen's window, jumping up and down.

"It's perfect!" she called back to us. "It's perfect! It's perfect!"

We clustered around to see what she'd found in the window. It was a box of chalk—all colors— each piece in a little card-board cradle in the box. There was a lot of dust on it, and the card above it said twenty-five cents. I noticed that the orange and brown pieces were slightly cracked in a few places, but overall, Shelley was right. Everybody knew Brenda was good in art, and this looked like the perfect gift.

And on top of that, Mr. Hempen marked it down to fifteen cents for us when I pointed out to him the broken pieces. We also bought a sack of jelly beans for Brenda, which came to forty-five cents.

"Now we need to make a card," Kate said on the way back to Shelley's. "I've got some yellow construction paper. We can make it at my house."

That card was amazingly hard to make. I mean, what do you say to someone with a dead father? Finally, after a bunch of tries, we just made a smiley face on the front in red and put HELLO on the inside in rainbow colors.

Brenda came back to school on Monday, but nobody knew what to say to her. In fact, everybody was kind of quiet that day, more like in Sunday school than in regular school. John Frank didn't even try to take my banana.

At recess, Kate and Shelley and Marla and I got together and decided to present the chalk and jelly beans to Brenda as a group.

"What do we say?" asked Marla, whispering, though there wasn't anyone near us at the time.

I looked at my three best friends standing there in a semicircle, looking at me. Marla, with her dark brown hair and eyes to match, her pretty quiet way of smiling all the time. Perky, excited Shelley, with her black eyes and bitten nails. Kate, her socks falling, as usual, and her long red hair pulled back into a ponytail that kept slipping, letting strands of hair fly out. They were all waiting for me to give them directions.

"That's a silly question," I told them. "We'll say what we'll say, that's all."

They nodded their heads solemnly, and we turned to walk together toward the bike racks where Brenda sat on a bench by herself. When we were there, standing around her, nobody said anything, and I felt my neck burning and wished Marla would speak up. Then I remembered that I had the card, and we had decided to give her that first, then the chalk, then the jelly beans.

"Hi, Brenda," I said. "Here. We made you this."

"And we got you these," said Marla. "The box isn't in very good shape, but only two pieces are cracked."

Then Kate handed her the jelly beans. The top of the white sack looked damp and crumpled where Kate had been clutching it.

Brenda just looked at us and at the heap our gifts made on the bench beside her. Nobody said anything. I began to wish the bell would ring. I decided something final needed to be said to bring the presentation to a quick close, and since the others were watching me from the sides of their eyes, I guessed I'd better say it.

"Well, we just got you this stuff, so here it is."

"Why?" asked Brenda.

The bell rang, finally.

When I got home that afternoon I decided to turn my rabbit loose. It was too complicated wondering every morning if he had grown overnight. I just didn't want to have to worry that I would miss the point where he was grown and keep him too long. Everything suddenly seemed complicated.

I took his cage to the edge of the clover field and left him there. I figured he would try to follow me home when I tilted up the basket, so I ran as fast as I could. But when I looked back over my shoulder, he was hopping away, into the field.

Marla said they just do that, and I shouldn't take it personally.

3 _Marla and Me_

If you look south of our big barn, way on past the two silos and then across the milo fields, you can sort of see Marla's house. Her dad has nearly nine hundred acres, mostly in row crops. Actually, you can't really see Marla's house but you can see the cedar fencerow that grows along the edge of her backyard.

Marla and I haven't always been best friends, not like some people who seem to link up together in kindergarten, or something. Our farms are close, but Shelley and Kate and a few other kids live within bike-riding distance too. So it's not like we were especially thrown together or stuck with each other, or anything like that.

Marla and I became best friends kind of suddenly, two falls ago, when we were just starting fifth grade. The summer before that I hadn't liked her a bit, with good reason.

A whole bunch of us ran around together that summer—the one between fourth and fifth grade—gathering on our bikes in peoples' yards to play stuff like clubhouse and jumprope. But our favorite thing to do was to put on plays.

Now, I don't like to brag, but the whole idea of putting on plays that summer was mine to begin with. And I usually came up with the play too. My grandmother says I am very creative. My mother says I must be careful to listen to other peoples' ideas too. She says I have a tendency to be bossy.

"Just think, always, before you speak, Jens," she's always telling me.

"I don't know why you're telling *me* that," I said back to her once last summer. "I'm always, always thinking! Why don't you ever tell Roger things like that he's bossy?"

I ran up to my room then, just furious, though far in the back of my mind I guess I realized my remark about Roger was a little farfetched. After all, he was only six months old at the time, and I guess it's practically impossible for someone that young to be truly bossy, although Roger certainly manages to keep Mama hopping.

Anyway, I usually came up with the plays that summer before last. The first one we did was *The Wizard of Oz*.

"Okay, who's going to be what?" I asked. There

was Kate and Marla and Marla's little brother, Fred, and another neighborhood boy named Carl Junior who was a real pest. Shelley wasn't there that day; I forget why.

Nobody said anything for a long time. As usual, they seemed to be waiting for me to give them directions. That is what my mother doesn't understand. How can you not be bossy when people are just standing around like chickens, expecting it?

"Okay, then," I said with a big sigh. "Marla will be the Scarecrow, and Fred will be the Tin Man. We can get some aluminum foil—I can sneak it from our kitchen. And Kate will make a good Lion with her big red hair. Carl Junior, you can be the Witch first, then switch to the Wizard at the very end. But if you set off one single firecracker, you have to go home, and I mean it. We want this to be a good play, not just a piece of junk. And I'll be Dorothy, I guess."

"I think Marla should be Dorothy," Kate said then. "She's the pretty one."

"Let's vote on it," piped Fred. "It's a free country!"

Fred was six years old that summer, and said that about any situation. In kindergarten they teach you the pledge to the flag and tell you all sorts of stuff about being in a free country. It had definitely impressed Fred.

"If that's what the rest of you want, then fine," I said reasonably, though the unfairness of the situation made me swallow hard. First they wait for me to make their decisions, then they find all kinds of fault with what I suggest.

"All in favor of Marla for Dorothy, raise your right hand," Kate said.

Everybody raised their hand. Carl Junior raised both of his, just to get attention.

"Hands down. Now, all in favor of Jens, raise your right hand." Carl Junior again raised both hands. Nobody else voted for me. I had intended to vote for myself, but was too embarrassed when nobody else did.

"Marla has it by a landslide," said Kate, and everybody yelled and clapped.

I don't remember too much else about that day, or the rest of the next two weeks when we practiced. We performed the play for our mothers and for Carl Junior's twin baby sisters. But the fun had gone out of it, as far as I was concerned.

I was the Scarecrow and gave it my all, considering how miscast I was. But Marla stole the show. Well, who wouldn't have, when they had the very main part to work with?

The next play I came up with was *Cinderella*. Marla was chosen by vote to be Cinderella. The next was *Alice in Wonderland*. Marla was chosen as Alice. That time, I was the Talking Caterpillar. By then, we were voting, at Fred's suggestion, for all the parts, and that's what they voted on for me. After I'd thought of the play and everything!

So I decided to wash my hands of the whole thing.

"Just let them come up with a play by themselves if they think they're so smart," I told my mother. "If they think Marla is so wonderful and I'm nothing but a fat old worm, just let them wait till doomsday for *her* to come up with a play. That's the hard part."

Mama and I were sitting on the porch swing at the time, shelling peas. It was dark enough that I didn't try to wipe the tears from my cheeks but just let them drip into the bowl of peas on my lap. Eventually I had to wipe my nose on my sleeve though, and when I did Mama looked my way quickly and put her arm around my shoulders.

"Oh, Jens," she said, "Marla's a cute, sweet girl. But you mustn't be jealous of her. You never need to be jealous of anybody."

Jealous? Me? This was another example of the times my mother and I didn't even seem to be remotely related. I had just explained to her that it was everybody's stupidity I was worried about, and here she had come up with some weird idea that had nothing to do with that. Besides, she was so beautiful herself, with her dark hair and pale, delicate skin, that how could she possibly know how it felt to be plain old average me?

"I'm not going over to Shelley's to practice tomorrow," I told her, giving her one more chance to understand. "I may not go anywhere the rest of this whole crummy summer!"

This seemed like a fairly safe threat, since school was starting the next week. When my mother didn't answer, I ran into the house and went upstairs and threw myself down on my bed. I would stay upstairs till I starved. That would teach my mother to understand me.

The next day I didn't go to Shelley's. I hung around the house instead, fixing things up. For quite a while I had been noticing how Mama didn't have the couch pillows or the plants on the mantel or the magazines on the endtable by the couch organized right. I set about changing them. When that was done, I attempted something harder. I replaced the dull crocheted tablecloths she had around on the dining room and coffee tables with cloths which I designed and cut from an old sheet, and decorated with Magic Markers.

"Jens," Mama said late that afternoon, "don't you think it's about time you forgot about this silly quarrel you have with the other kids and got some fresh air?"

"I'm too busy," I told her, moving Grandma's old clock from the mantel to place a cloth under it. It looked much better now, much less plain, with orange daisies and a rainbow to show it up. I should have started this project long before, I kept thinking.

"Jens, I really think it's time you left the home decorating to me," Mama said, her voice tight this time. "I think you need to get outside."

Well, if that didn't cut it. It's one thing when your friends don't appreciate your hard work picking plays, but when your own mother doesn't recognize all you've done for her! Furious, I set out on my bike, but not for Shelley's house, where I knew those ungrateful people were at this very moment trying unsuccessfully to come up with a play idea.

Instead, I headed for the school yard, clear in Iola. The school was farther away than I had ever ridden on my bike at that time and I hadn't asked permission to go there because I didn't think I'd get it. Besides, I was too mad at Mama to ask her anything.

All the way to the school I pedalled twice as fast as usual, shaking my head with disbelief that everybody could be so blind. Everybody! And then I started to cry again for the second time in just two days.

I was exhausted when I finally reached the big black playground surrounding the red brick school—exhausted and totally angry and desperate. I had to do something, something to show them all.

Well, once I got my breath back and looked

around the playground, it didn't take me two seconds to come up with the perfect thing.

It was almost amazing. It looked like the playground equipment had just been painted that morning. It gleamed silver, hurting my eyes, looking like a forest of just-landed spacecraft. And under each of the swing bars lay a puddle of silver paint, just as if I'd ordered it up.

"No, you really can't do that," I told myself as I stirred the shining paint in a small puddle with my finger. But then I looked hard at the puddle at my feet and imagined it was a mirror. And in that mirror I saw the image of little goody-two-shoes Marla, who even my own mother thought was just so sweet and perfect it was nauseating. My own mother!

Well, I could show them that Marla wasn't as perfect as they all thought. I looked all around me and saw no one. In the hot August air not even a tree leaf was stirring.

Very carefully, trying not to drip on my new sneakers, I bent down and got more of the gooey paint on my finger. Then, leaving a track of drips across the pavement, I ran to the front of the school and right beside the big double front doors found a clear area of red brick.

It took me seven or eight trips between the swing pole puddles and the front of the school to get all five letters of Marla's name printed in big capital letters. They really glowed against that red brick. I could see them from clear down the street. In fact, M A R L A was the first thing anyone would notice driving past the school from now on out.

I wiped my finger off as well as I could on the grass in the ditch and started back home, looking over my shoulder again as I turned the corner that would hide the school from sight. Sure enough, the big silver letters were visible from this distance of nearly three blocks.

By the time I got home, and it was nearly dark, I knew Mama would be furious. On top of that, now that I had had a strenuous afternoon of bike riding and painting to settle things in my mind, I was feeling kind of sick about the whole thing. Anger is fun while it lasts, in a weird kind of way. But the feeling you get when it's gone is lousy. Especially if you've painted someone's name on the school building in eight-inch-high silver letters.

"I don't feel so good," I mumbled, hoping Mama would decide not to start with the lecture I could see in her eyes as she stood holding the screen door open for me.

Immediately, she frowned more deeply, but I could tell it was a frown of concern, not the kind of frown that leads to a fight. She put a hand on my forehead.

"You're feverish," she said. "Into bed with you, and I'll be up in a minute."

When she had put a cool cloth on my head and

bustled over me and finally left the room, I lay staring at the ceiling, miserable. In the middle of the night I got up and went to the bathroom and vomited.

"Daddy, is there any way to get paint off bricks?" I asked at breakfast the next morning, trying to sound casual, though I couldn't keep a little shake out of my voice.

"Well, sweetie, if it's lead-based paint, and it's dried on there real good, I guess it would take a whole awful lot of wire brushing to do a bit of good. *If* that would even work. Depends on how porous the bricks are, partly. Whether it's really soaked in. Why do you ask?"

I had been hoping he'd say it would wash off, or maybe even rain off.

"Excuse me," I whispered, and ran upstairs to vomit in the bathroom again.

That was the Saturday beginning the worst weekend of my whole life. School was going to start the next Monday, which meant I had about forty-eight hours full of minutes, each one crammed with the horror of what I had done. I spent the entire two days lying on my bed, thinking endlessly about the coming catastrophe. I knew about how it would go. Mr. Thompson would drive to the school early Monday morning to unlock things, a big smile on his face as he thought about the bright new school year. Then he would see the silver paint, the hideous glaring letters, and maybe he would die of the awfulness of the thing right then and there. His forehead would hit the horn in his car, bringing folks running from all directions.

"What in the world happened to poor Mr. Thompson?" they would ask each other, then they would see the big shocking silver name themselves, and their hands would fly to their mouths in horror.

Or maybe Mr. Thompson would live, would grimly let himself into the building and would begin planning a punishment bad enough for the person who had done this terrible, unbelievable thing.

"Bring that Marla to me," he would hiss to Mrs. Harkness, the fifth grade teacher. "I'll teach her a lesson she'll never forget!"

And Marla would be dragged from our class, one of the custodians holding each arm, while I sat watching, a coward to the core.

"Just cut out your worrying," I tried to tell myself occasionally those awful two days. "Remember, Little Miss Perfect deserves whatever's coming to her."

But whenever I thought that, I only felt sicker.

By Monday morning I was totally numb, a zombie. I couldn't smile, couldn't listen to anything anybody was telling me, could barely talk myself. I just wanted to fall into a pit somewhere.

And then I had a hopeful thought.

"I guess they're still having school this year, aren't they?" I eagerly asked my mother. "I mean, you haven't heard on the radio or anything about them changing their plans, deciding just to forget it or anything, have you?"

She looked at me over her coffee cup, her eyes slitted.

"Jens, is something wrong? I mean, I know first-day jitters are a part of going to school. But you're acting a little under the weather. Are you still sick?"

My heart leaped. Of course, that was the answer! If I said I was sick, as gross as I was looking, Mama would let me stay home!

I opened my mouth to tell her I felt terrible, but the words came out wrong.

"No . . . no, I'm okay," I said, picking up my lunchbox and going listlessly out the door, toward the bus. I could see it coming down our road like a big yellow monster, just waiting to swallow me up.

After the torture of waiting all weekend for doom to fall, I didn't have long at all to wait on Monday.

We had only been in class about half an hour and had just met Mrs. Harkness and had our first roll taken, when Mr. Thompson's secretary appeared in the doorway of our classroom.

"Excuse me, Mrs. Harkness," Miss Titterly whispered, her tiny frame quivering with sorrow and nervousness at what she was doing. "But Mr.

Thompson would very much like to see Marla Stevens in his office for a moment, please."

In spite of my own problems, I couldn't help feeling sorry for Miss Titterly. She was the type of old lady who loved the part of her job that involved making dinosaur nametags for the kindergarteners, but she hated this "jailer" part of her job.

Everybody got deathly silent. They had all seen Marla's name on the school by then, of course. It had been all anybody had talked about all morning, whispering and giggling. They all knew that poor Marla was in for it, was about to walk that long mile to the office with only Miss Titterly's tiny frame to support her.

Marla got up, everybody's eyes following her, and walked to the front of the room. I could see that her face was pale. My lips and tongue felt like they were made of rubber. I tried to speak, to stop things, but I couldn't. And then, just before she went out the door, Marla turned and looked straight at me for just half a second. My heart fell to the bottom of my feet and I felt hollow.

"Now, class, let's get back to work. Please take out your new English book, and turn to the first page," Mrs. Harkness said, as though the sky hadn't just fallen. We all fumbled in our desks. I grabbed a book—I'm not sure which one—and numbly opened it.

"Mark, will you please read, beginning at the top of the page?" How could she talk so calmly?

Maybe she felt she had to create a diversion, keep up a lot of noise in the room so we wouldn't hear Marla's screams.

Mark began reading. A humming began and grew louder in my ears as he droned on.

"Thank you, Mark. Jens, will you please read the next two paragraphs?"

I tried to breathe right, but things were closed in my throat. "I . . . I . . ." the words in the strange book on my desk ran together, spun crazily.

"Jens, are you all right? Will you please ask someone for the place and then read? And from now on, please follow along!"

And then I was on my feet, hurrying to her desk. "I need to go talk to Mr. Thompson, Mrs. Harkness," I whispered urgently to her. And when she nodded, puzzled, I ran from the room, hearing giggles at my back.

The hall seemed to go on and on, getting longer the farther I ran, like in some horror movie. It took hours I thought but I finally reached the office at the foot of the stairs.

"Miss Titterly, I've got to tell Mr. Thompson something!" I shouted at her, and she began nodding quickly, her tight gray curls flopping up and down. I skidded past her desk to the inner office and knocked on the door.

"Just a moment, please. I'm with a student." Mr. Thompson's voice sounded amazingly calm, human even.

I knocked again. "But you're with the wrong student, Mr. Thompson," I called through the door.

Then he opened the door. I saw Marla sitting in the corner. She had her hands clasped in her lap, and it looked as though she might have been crying.

"Miss Tucker, come in please, and tell us what you have to say," Mr. Thompson said sternly. His voice was gruff and scary, but not nearly as scary as the voices in my head had become. He went back around and sat down behind his desk, pointing for me to sit in a chair by Marla.

"I did it," I said, surprised that my voice didn't shake. I felt relief flood over me at my words, even though the worst was to come. "I painted Marla's name on the school. Marla didn't have anything to do with it. She wasn't even anywhere around."

Marla looked up quickly, met my eyes, which I immediately dropped in shame.

My punishment from Mr. Thompson was to get the paint off the school. He said that he knew I wasn't usually the kind of person to do such a thing, and he thought I'd learned a big lesson, so he would go easy on me this time.

My parents didn't agree with his easiness. They grounded me for two months and went with me to apologize formally to Marla's whole family.

That was awful. Mrs. Stevens looked like she thought I should be ground into little pieces and fed to the pigs, though Mama said later she thought that was my imagination.

The next Saturday Daddy gave me a wire brush and half a bucket of paint remover stuff and offered to drive me to the school, but I asked him if I could ride my bike instead, and he said I could.

Anyway, I'd been working there for about an hour or so when Marla rode up behind me on her bike.

"Hi," she said, kind of halfway smiling, looking like she was scared or something.

"Come to gloat?" I spat out at her over my shoulder. I was ashamed for doing that, but my back hurt something awful already, and I'd hardly made a dent in the paint.

"No," she said quietly. "I just thought . . . thought maybe I could help."

I could hardly believe my ears but when I looked back over my shoulder at her, there were tears in her eyes.

"Why?" I asked, turning back around to stare at my wall. There were tears in my eyes too, but I'd be darned if I'd let her see.

"I don't know. I guess I just wish you liked me or something," she said. "Everybody thinks you're so smart and everything, and I know you think I'm really stupid, but I still don't know why you hate me about that."

Everybody thought I was smart? That was news to me. I stood up and faced her directly, tears running down my face.

"Well, everybody thinks you're Miss Perfect, with your cuteness and niceness and everything," I blubbered. "How do you think that makes me feel, when I think of the plays and everything?"

But though my words sounded like my heart was broken, that wasn't exactly the case. Marla had just told me that everybody thought I was smart, and that made a whole lot of things easier to take.

"I guess that made you feel pretty rotten," she answered. "I never thought about it before. I was just too jealous of your ideas and the way kids listen to you to think about it."

Her, jealous of *me*?

"But I was the one jealous of you," I admitted before I could stop myself. "I would give anything to look and act like you."

She ducked her head and looked embarrassed, then got off her bike and put her kickstand down.

"Which do you want me to use, the wire brush or the rags?" she asked.

And that was in the beginning of fifth grade, more than a year and a half ago, and we've been best friends ever since.

Which is why the hardest part of this whole thing for me is losing Marla.

4 *My Awful Teeth*

It was about two weeks after Brenda Miller's father died that I first noticed a horrible thing about my teeth. The two on top next to the middle ones had always been slightly crooked, but suddenly when I looked in the bathroom mirror one night I noticed they were heaving grotesquely to the side, more each minute.

"Oh, Jens, don't be so silly," Mama said when I showed her, which is why I never bother to show her anything.

I went back upstairs and checked again. Sure enough, they were worse than they had been minutes before. I decided to start pushing on them when I got a chance and settled at my desk to do my social studies homework while I pushed.

But when I opened my book, I found a note I'd

written to myself the night I heard my parents talking in the kitchen—the night Brenda Miller's father died.

"Don't forget—ask Marla what Daddy meant by the land eating us all alive," I'd written.

Well, that settled it. I had to talk to Marla immediately. Not only about my teeth, but about the note too.

"Mama, I've got to go somewhere!" I called on my way out through the family room, knowing she would stop me if I didn't build enough speed.

I didn't quite make it to the door.

"Whoa, young lady, it's dark outside! Just where do you need to go at this hour?"

"Mama! I've got to talk to Marla, right now!"

"But can't you just call her? You promised your father you'd help with chores in the morning before school, so you need to be getting to bed."

I was glad she'd taken that tack, because I had a pat answer for it that worked nearly every time.

"Miss Petrison's on the party line. Please?"

Mama has her share of frustration over getting the line away from Miss Petrison, so she gave in, as I'd been pretty sure she would.

"Be back in one hour, you hear? One hour."

I biked past the clover field, onto the gravel road. The sky was dark, but not the navy it turns later. It was a velvety purple, my favorite way for it to be.

The outbuildings—the two barns, chicken house, and silo—looked beautiful and mysterious, like ancient castles against the dark clouds. In the daylight they looked sort of scruffy, their red paint peeling, the wood warping in places. Daddy is always saying that paint and lumber will have to wait for better times.

For better times. Now why hadn't I ever really thought about what he meant by that? I thought of the note now in my jeans pocket that I'd written the night I heard him talking in the kitchen and I shivered.

Mrs. Stevens looked kind of stiff when she opened the door for me. "Well, hello there Jens. Kind of late to be out, isn't it?"

Since that thing with the name on the school, I've never been real sure that Mrs. Stevens likes me too well. But she's like most mothers and doesn't come right out and say it, if she doesn't.

"Hi, Mrs. Stevens. Is Marla around?"

"She's up in her room studying, but you girls don't visit too long, hear? School tomorrow."

I walked up the beige-carpeted stairway, so different from our rickety wooden stairs. Marla lives in a new colonial-style house with central heating and everything. I always wonder if Mama is envious when she has to keep our wood stoves filled in the dead of winter.

"Marla?" I knocked on her door, and heard her laughing. She was on the phone, I guessed. I never can get over the fact that Marla actually has a phone in her room, but she does.

I pushed the door on open and walked in and sat down on her lavendar bedspread, pulling my Nikes up under me and leaning with my elbows on my knees. Marla was sprawled on the floor, her long glossy brown hair around her head like a fan. She was still laughing at something the person on the phone was saying, and her even, shiny teeth glittered and shone. She raised one arm over her head to wave to me, upside down. I shrugged my shoulders and bobbed my head in an effort to get her to hurry.

"Well, listen John Frank, I better go," she said, smiling with those teeth for all she was worth. "See you tomorrow at school. Bye bye."

Let me tell you, shock set in and set in bad. I could barely move my mouth to close it.

"Jens, what in the world is the matter with you?" Marla asked, on her feet now, the picture of concern. Ha! "You look like you've just got a chicken bone caught in your throat."

"John . . . John Frank?" I managed to choke out. "You've actually been talking on the phone with John Frank Richardson?"

"He just called to ask a couple of things about our math assignment, that's all," she said, but I could tell from the color of her neck above her sweatshirt collar that she felt funny about it, as she definitely should have!

"After all the times I've told you I just can't stand him and all the times he's taken my bananas and everything, I just don't understand how you can talk to him like that!" I pretty much screamed at her.

"For Pete's sake, Jens, it was only to tell him a homework assignment."

"Oh? Oh? And I don't suppose there are boys in our class that he could have called to ask about that, is that what you're trying to tell me?" I replied, keeping myself collected and reasonable, though the unfairness of the whole situation was about to overwhelm me.

No, any way you looked at it it wasn't fair at all. I had been born with medium brown hair, medium blue eyes, medium height, and a medium build. I had medium freckles on my arms and no matter how much time I took in the bathroom in the morning if you asked someone how I looked overall they would probably tell you "medium." And now I had these impossible teeth to set off all the mediumness, and yet all Marla had to do was lie down on a stupid floor for her hair to fan out that way and for John Frank to be calling her and everything, making her perfect teeth flash. And it had been me who had given up all those bananas! Me!

"I have to get home. I can't imagine why I came over here in the first place," I told her stiffly, standing and heading for the door. "It certainly wasn't to interrupt your oh-so-important conversation."

"Jens?" she said, looking hurt. "Hey, don't leave. And don't be mad, okay?"

She really did look like she honestly didn't know why I was upset. These ultra-sweet people can be so blind sometimes.

"Good-bye, Marla," I said coldly, closing the door behind me. I ran down the stairs and biked home fast as I could.

And I decided then and there that if that was how Marla was going to be I would never—never!—ask her opinion about my teeth.

As it turned out, it was just as well that I didn't get a chance to talk to Marla about my second worry—the one about what my father had said. Because the next morning, in the milk barn, Daddy talked to me about it himself.

I have always loved helping with the milking, once I'm up. It's not easy getting out of bed at 4:30, though, and going out into the icy darkness, your big rubber boots sinking into the mud of the barn-yard. We call it mud, anyway, to make ourselves feel better. Well, it is mud, partly. Anyway, some-body goes on horseback to get the milk cows from the far pasture, and the cows huddle in the lot like ships, dark and solid in the gloom. You have to be careful they don't step on your toes. Their breath makes a fog over the whole area in the winter and early spring.

We bring them into the milking stalls two by two. First you wash the udders with warm soapy water, then you attach the stainless steel milkers and watch the foamy liquid travel through the plastic tubing to the big milk tank in the other room. When you take off the milkers they make a whooshing sound of lost suction. I always wonder if that hurts, or tickles. Then you skim the last of the milk from the cow by hand and let her have her feed as you do it. A couple of them always kick. Daddy says every herd is bound to have kickers.

A long time ago, that first summer when Daddy had me help, I found that there's a knothole in the wood of the milk barn that lines up exactly with a real bright morning star. There's no more peaceful feeling than looking out that knothole and making a wish on that star while the sky begins to turn from navy to royal blue to day, and the milking machine whirs behind you.

"Be careful, Jenser, that cow has a sore udder. She may kick," Daddy told me that morning as I started on my first cow. But I had already seen the inflammation and knew to be careful.

"Is this one Gladys?" I asked him. I used to have every single cow named, but that was a year or so ago. Other things have been on my mind since, and I'd given up and pretty much gone by the numbers stapled in their ears, like everybody else does.

"I believe it might be at that," he said, smiling over his shoulder at me.

I smiled back, not even thinking about how awful my teeth looked when I did. Around Daddy, I don't have to worry about things like that.

Mama and I are like from different planets, but Daddy and I understand each other. Mama is slim and delicate and beautiful. Daddy and I are both medium everything, but on him it looks good. He's big and quiet and safe, and the most handsome man I've ever seen.

"Come over here a minute, Jenser," he said that morning when we had finished the cows, before we started cleaning up. He moved to a big tool box in the corner of the room and pushed aside a pile of feed sacks to make a sitting place for the two of us. He took off his Corn Producers hat and used it to brush off a cleaner place for me.

I went happily to sit beside him, leaning my head back against his denim, tobacco-smelling jacket. He smokes a pipe, but not in the house. Mama won't let him.

"Honey, I want to tell you some things that I think you're old enough to understand," he said quietly.

I swallowed hard, somehow knowing this

wouldn't be good. I felt in my bones it had something to do with the peeling paint on the outbuildings having to wait for better times, and with the scared feeling I'd had in the far back of my mind since I'd overheard him talking about the land eating us. I have a trick I sometimes do, which is to keep telling myself that in a scary situation you only have to face things one second at a time, one second at a time. I started doing that in the milk barn with Daddy that morning—just counting off the seconds, wishing for this talk to be over. I liked things just the way they were, but sensed they were about to change.

"Jens, do you remember last fall, when we had all that rain in October and the soybeans started sprouting before we could get in the fields to cut them? We lost that crop, and we lost part of the corn. And I told you then we'd have to really be careful. I think there were half a dozen farmers in this county that went under at that time—half a dozen families that lost their farms."

I nodded. I remembered. A couple of kids in our class moved away. Their farms sold at auction that November. The papers were crowded with sale bills for several weeks.

"Well, sweetheart, your mother and I said to ourselves at that time that it would take a good harvest this year to keep us going," he went on, his voice slower than it had been. He ran a hand through his hair and cleared his throat. "And, well, we also counted on the pigs we sold this winter to get us through."

"But the pigs did great!" I said, feeling excitement go through the gloom that had settled over me. "Don't you remember? We hardly lost any, and they were all good weight."

He put his arm around my shoulders and squeezed hard, then didn't let go.

"Jens, try to understand what I'm about to tell you. The pigs did great, like you say. But so did everyone else's in Missouri, and in the whole Midwest. There was a glut in the market, and we didn't even get back what it cost us to raise them. Jennifer, things are looking . . ."

He didn't finish the sentence, just gripped my shoulder tighter and dropped his head and cleared his throat again. My heart beat fast with helplessness and confusion. And then I saw a ray of hope that he'd missed.

"But Daddy, we can still have a great harvest this year, and things will be fine, like they used to be!"

He dropped his arm from my shoulders and stood up, taking a few steps away from me. And with his back toward me and his shoulders slumped he talked in that same awful voice I'd heard him use the night Brenda's father died.

"Honey, right now we don't have enough money or credit to buy the seed and fertilizer we need to finish the planting, let alone to harvest next fall. We've got one slim hope. The government has come up with a plan to buy up milk herds, to force prices up for the dairy farmers that stay in the business. I've sold the herd, Jens. They'll pick it up later this week. Maybe the money will keep us going a while longer."

I felt like I'd been kicked in the stomach, but I had to know a little more, no matter how much my voice was shaking, no matter how much I wanted this to be over.

"But Mama says the milk check pays the grocery bill," I said, amazed that he could have overlooked that fact.

He walked to the door, his back still toward me, and bent to inspect a place where the wood was splintered in the wall.

"Well, Jens, something else will have to come along to pay for that now," he said, so long after I had spoken that I thought he hadn't heard me. Then he took the big red handkerchief from his back overall pocket and blew his nose and left the barn, walking into the fog of the early morning.

5 *Iola*

When Daddy was gone I looked back out the knothole. I could barely still see the wishing star, now nearly faded out by the light of dawn, and I had the strong feeling that if I could think of just the right wish things might be all right again.

I'd never wished anything important before—just to get a certain thing for Christmas and stuff like that. I'd thought about wishing Roger would be a girl before he was born, but I decided at the last minute I didn't really care if he turned out to be a girl or a boy. So that didn't count.

And now, when I desperately needed to think of a wish, I couldn't. I couldn't wish for a good harvest, because Daddy had just said we didn't have the money for planting. I couldn't wish milk prices would go up, because we were losing the herd.

While I was wondering, the sky got lighter and the star disappeared. I looked for a long time at the hole of light blue where it had been, but when I felt tears throbbing in my throat I scolded myself angrily.

"Don't be such a stupid baby," I yelled at myself, so loud a bunch of barnswallows took off from a hay bale in surprise and flew to the rafters. "It's time you quit believing in wishes and started acting your age!"

My eyes felt hot, and I ran out to the cool of the cow lot, searching for Gladys.

It was light enough to tell her by the number in her ear—21. I put my arms around her neck and hugged her, taking deep breaths of the sharp, cold air. I was so ashamed now that I had quit naming the cows. I felt like a traitor. Would they blame me for what was coming?

I didn't feel real, walking through the mud to the back porch. In the bathroom I kicked my barn clothes toward the hamper and stepped under the shower. And it was there, with the hard, hot water drumming on my head, that my numbness began to thaw and I had an awful thought. As if finding out we were losing our herd wasn't bad enough, this morning I'd have to ride the bus with John Frank and Marla!

"Mama!" I cried, rushing downstairs and into the kitchen with a towel clutched around me, my hair streaming behind me. "Mama, please let me ride my bike to school today!"

"Jens?" she said slowly, turning from the stove to take a step toward me. Roger, in his playpen by the refrigerator, flapped his fat arms and laughed. "Jens, is anything . . . wrong?"

"Please, Mama? It's a matter of life and death!"

"But I thought you said you were too old for bike riding in town now. I thought you said . . ."

"Mama!"

"All right! All right! Anything!" She flung up her hands in that way she has when I ask her things, but then, when I had started running back upstairs, leaving a trail of drips from under my towel, she called me.

"Jens?" she said softly. "Come here a minute."

I came back down, wondering if I was in trouble for dripping.

But she took my head between her hands and looked into my eyes for a minute, then pulled me toward her and hugged me, rocking me back and forth in her arms. I squeezed my eyes shut, and my throat got tight again.

"Baby, everything will work out, one way or the other," she said. "Believe me?"

I nodded against her shoulder. I certainly was not a baby, but at that particular moment, I didn't feel like correcting her.

*   *   *

I rode into Iola along the back gravel roads. It took a few minutes longer, and my jeans and sweatshirt got a little dusty, but it was worth it not to chance seeing the bus on the blacktop.

I was at the edge of town when I saw Betty and Petey Thurman up ahead of me, pulling Petey's rusty wagon down the middle of the dusty road. I started to duck down Iola's one and only side street, but Betty had already seen me. She was waving wildly with her arms, flagging me down.

This was all I needed this morning, I thought miserably. Just exactly all I needed.

Betty and Petey moved to Iola a little over a year ago. They live in one of the houses at the edge of town, one of the three that were partly set on fire when a grain silo nearby exploded several years go. Those three houses—shacks really—are vacant most of the time. But somebody tries to live in one of them occasionally, somebody drifting through or down on their luck. The upstairs of Betty and Petey's house doesn't even have glass in the windows.

The week Betty and Petey moved into town, I heard Mrs. Hempen talking to Mrs. Creel at the check-out counter in the store. "More trash come to town," Mrs. Creel was saying. I told Mama about that later, and she looked angry and told me I was not to repeat such things, ever. Still, she did tell me that Betty and Petey's mama had a drinking problem, and that their daddy ran out on them before they moved here.

I know for a fact that their mama is hardly ever at home, and once when I asked Betty where she was she said "mama don't tell me her business."

Anyway, there they were, flagging me down on what was already one of the worst mornings of my life.

"Hi Betty. Hi Pete," I said, braking to a stop beside them and balancing on my left leg, trying not to sound too friendly. "Why aren't you guys heading toward school?"

As if I didn't know. Betty and Petey went to school if and when they pleased, about half the time or less. But I had to say something to them, and that seemed like a safe thing to say so I could take off without getting into a big discussion. But they ignored the question.

"I like them shoes," said Betty, leaning toward my right Nike on the pedal of my bike. "I don't have no shoes like that."

Embarrassment crawled up my neck like a spider, and I felt my cheeks begin to burn. I tried not to look at Betty's too-long skirt with half of its hem hanging down, unstitched. Or her ratty orange plastic thongs. They were that kind you sometimes see in discount stores at the end of the summer for about a dollar a pair and they were the only thing I'd ever seen her have on her feet, even in the dead of winter. Of course, then she wore gray socks with them, men's socks. I guessed her father had left them behind when he ran off.

"Thanks," I choked out, my face feeling like plastic when I smiled. "I like them too."

"Can I have a quarter?" asked Petey, sticking out his small, grubby hand. His nose was running, as usual. There was a long, sticky line of it along his left shirt sleeve too.

"No, Petey, I don't have any money," I said automatically. That wasn't hard to do any more, though at first it had been. Everybody's mothers told them right off the bat—when Betty and Petey had first moved to Iola and started begging—that we didn't have any business giving them money.

"Hey, could be those shoes would fit me," Betty said then. Her greasy blonde hair was falling in her eyes, dull green eyes that had seen lots of things— many of them, I knew, not good. Her skin was pale, and she smelled awful. I knew she was older than Marla and Shelley and Kate and me, but she was put in the sixth grade. It hardly mattered what grade she was in, she came so seldom.

Petey was five, Betty said, though he looked the size of a three or four-year-old. He spent his days pulling his wagon along the streets of Iola, hoping people would put stale donuts or used clothes in it. He usually begged alone, but Betty was always someplace nearby.

"I . . . I don't imagine they would," I told her, swallowing hard. "I have funny feet, real weird. My shoes hardly fit anybody else, ever."

She stared at me, her dull eyes drilling into mine with their misery. I wanted nothing in the world so bad as to jump back on my bike and to pedal for all I was worth away from them, but she held me with those eyes of hers. I was scared to death of her poorness.

"I could try them at least, I guess," she said, moving closer to me. I could smell her hair. I was terrified, and pushed my kickstand up.

"I've got to go, Betty. See you."

My heart was beating way too fast the rest of the few blocks to school.

"Hey, where were you this morning? I saved your seat on the bus. I thought you must be sick or something." Marla was out of breath from running to catch me in the hall before the bell.

Now, the thing you have to remember about Marla is her niceness. With anybody else, it would have been impossible to believe they were so blind, and didn't understand that when you talked on the phone to someone your best friend hated, your best friend would be very, very hurt. But Marla was so sweet and nice that it probably went right past her.

So I decided to just let it go, at least for now.

"I just wanted to, you know, ride my bike this

morning," I told her nonchalantly, hanging my jacket and backpack on one of the hooks outside our room.

"Why didn't you call me? I could have ridden with you," she said, following me to my desk.

"I didn't think of it," I said, still wanting to punish her just a little, tiny bit. "Sorry, it just slipped my mind I guess."

"That's okay," she said, sounding hurt.

"By the way, did John Frank happen to ride the bus today?" I asked nonchalantly.

"Yeah, he sat by me, since your seat was empty."

I think I managed to get through the next few seconds with amazing calmness and control, all things considered.

"Excuse me, Marla," I said evenly, picking up my books and walking to the front of the room where Miss Horton stood writing the assignments for the day on the board. The final bell rang as I approached her, and tapped her lightly on the shoulder.

"Miss Horton, I really don't feel very well. My mother was worried sick about me, and begged me to stay home, but I just hated to miss a single day of class. Still, I think I better leave now, after all."

She turned toward me with concern in her eyes, and bewilderment. "But will anybody be home to come pick you up, Jens?"

"Luckily, it so happens I rode my bike today," I told her, "so I had just better hurry and go now, before I feel worse and vomit on the floor or something."

I'd added that part about vomiting so I could get out of there quick. My cool, calm act had lasted about as long as I could get it to last.

"Well, if you're sure you can make . . ." she began, but I was already hurrying for the door, my composure about stretched as far as it would stretch.

In the hall I banged my hand along the wall and kicked at things furiously as I ran, tears making me practically blind.

I didn't really care if I wiped out on my bike, so sure enough, I did. A few blocks from school, in the middle of Iola's pitiful shopping district, I got too close to the curb and went over with a sickening, scraping sound. I was positive I'd demolished my right leg but when I kicked my bike off and looked down, a pathetically small area of red showed through the torn denim on my knee, nothing more.

Still, I sat there in the road, crying and bleeding and wishing a car would just come along and finish me off. That would show them all. But fat chance—cars go down Iola's Main Street at about the rate of one an hour.

What did show up was Jack Shire. He came rushing out of the building where he stores those six convertibles of his, and which happened to be the building I'd wiped out in front of.

"Jens Tucker, is that you?" he asked, crouching beside me. "Are you all right and everything, girl?"

Mr. Shire must be about sixty and has one glass eye and a habit of wearing the same overalls all summer and then just adding a flannel shirt and wearing them all winter too. He says he has chewed tobacco since the age of five and still has half his teeth so that proves it's good for you. He tells everybody he sleeps standing in a corner to make him live to be a hundred. He raises mules and chickens for a living on the hard scrabble few acres he shares with his elderly mother, Mrs. Elvetta Shire. But his true love, everybody knows, more than his mules or his tobacco or anything, is his convertibles.

Lots of folks, my parents included, call him "a trifle peculiar." Which is why I didn't know if I was supposed to be talking to him, all alone in the street and all.

"Whoa, girl. Them spokes is bad busted," he said, shaking his head and clucking his tongue. "Chain's off too. Come inside whiles I fix her up."

"Well, thanks Mr. Shire, but I don't know if I should be . . ."

"Aw, come on in! I ain't worried about you messing things up, girl! You can't barely help it if you's clumsy!"

He laughed out loud then and pushed the door of his old bank-building-turned-convertible-garage wide open for me. I'd never in my wildest dreams thought I'd ever be inside there and I knew my mother would have a screaming fit if she knew. So I decided to compromise and just stand there in the doorway, by the street, so I wouldn't hurt his feelings.

The big, hollow building was falling apart on the inside, just as it was on the outside. The six huge cars were parked bumper to bumper, three on each side, and some of the old bank furniture—rotten desks and green filing cabinets covered with rust—were crammed against the walls. Ivy was growing through the cracks in the walls, and even into the back seat of one of the cars, a long turquoise one with huge fins and gobs of chrome. Most of the ceiling was gone, collapsed. Big hunks of plaster filled the seats of most of the cars.

"Ain't they beauties?" Mr. Shire called up to me from the back of the huge room where he was working over my bike under a bare, hanging light bulb, the only light in the place.

"Yes," I told him truthfully. I was totally impressed now that I'd seen the building from the inside. The six cars reminded me, somehow, of mermaids, hopelessly beached and out of their element but still gorgeous in a strange sort of way. The shadowy gloom of the room was part of it, making everything seem underwater and mysterious. "Do any of them run?" I asked him.

"Well, not so's you'd notice," he answered, hefting my bike off his filthy worktable and starting back toward me with it. "I fully intend to fix them up one of these days though, and sell them as collectors' items. They are what could be called my ace in the hole, my fortune. Worth their weight in gold, I figure they are."

I thought back to times I'd heard my father laugh about Mr. Jack Shire, say that those convertibles had been sitting there for thirty years and would sit there a hundred more. Saying they were worthless pieces of junk, not salvageable even for someone who knew what he was doing, which Jack Shire, my father said, more than likely did not.

Oh well, it really didn't matter. I could see that Jack Shire would never sell those cars even if he did get them to run.

"There she be," Mr. Shire said. I looked down at my bike, saw the chain tight, the spokes straight as new.

"Wow, thanks. Really." I pushed back out into the clear spring air from his musty, cavelike workshop of strange cars. "I really, really appreciate this."

"Well, you stop by again, and next time have a chaw, hear?" He took his tobacco from his pocket, smiling his wide, gap-toothed smile.

Down the block, I looked back over my shoulder and waved. He still stood there, like some ancient guardian of a secret world.

6   *The Auction*

When you're coming to our house down the blacktop from Iola, there's a certain place where you can stop under a big mulberry tree and get your breath. And from that exact spot the house and barns and silo look pretty as a postcard. Up half a mile closer you notice the flaking paint and ruts in the drive and all the broken machinery that Daddy keeps for parts clustered outside the big barn. Things don't look so pretty and perfect then. Still, I think that first look from under the mulberry tree has always been the truest one.

When I left Jake Shire's, wondering if my knee would stiffen up so much before I got home that I would have to walk my bike partway, I found myself looking forward more than usual to my stop under the mulberry tree. I had so much to think out, and that seemed like the place to do it.

When I reached the tree, it was amazing how much things had come together in my mind. I realized that all I had to do was make a list of things and I would be halfway to losing the awful confused feeling I had had growing in me all week.

I took a piece of notebook paper from my backpack, my bad knee resting on the grass, my back against the good old mulberry tree. I centered the title I'd decided on and began to write.

Things I Have to Worry About
(1) my horrible teeth
(2) losing the herd
(3) John Frank being so nice to Marla
(4) what Daddy said about the land eating us

I shivered when I wrote that last thing. I still didn't really know what it meant, but every time I thought about that night, when I had heard my parents talking, I felt scared.

A car was coming—I could hear it a long way off on the blacktop. It turned out to be Mama and Roger, in the pickup, the back full of grocery sacks.

"Jennifer Melissa Tucker, whatever are you doing out of school?" she called out Roger's window over the noise of the truck's bad muffler. She was leaning out Roger's window, toward me. Roger's fat, smiling face was under hers, and he stuck one tiny arm out the window and pumped it up and down, grabbing for me.

"I was sick," I began, getting up stiffly and limping toward them, hoping Mama would notice the blood on my knee. "And I got hurt, on my bike."

Her face relaxed a little, but she shook her head.

"Well, you get on home. If you're sick enough to miss school, you have no business lollygagging under the mulberry tree. Leave your bike there for your father to pick up later, and hop in the truck."

"I can ride. I feel okay," I told her.

And with an elaborate sigh and shrug of her shoulders she rolled up Roger's window and they went on down the road toward home.

Sometimes I wished I was Roger. He had eight teeth now, all of them straight. And he was so lovable that no one could resist him, specially not Mama.

I sat back in the grass and added one last thing to the list before I folded it up and stuck it in my bluejean pocket, then limped to my bike and headed the rest of the way home.

That night a wonderful thing happened that almost made up for the rottenness of the rest of the day. Daddy invited me to go to the Richards County Auction with him!

"Jim, you're not serious," said Mama, glaring at him across the dinner table.

"I reckon she's old enough, Greta," he said slowly, and I could tell he was trying not to smile. "How old are you now Jenser? Eleven?"

He knew very well I was twelve, going on thirteen, so I just rolled my eyes at him. But I had to smile too, I was so excited. Everybody wanted to go to the auction.

"But that filthy place is not suitable for a child," Mama said, more firmly. "Those old men spitting on the floor, not to mention the language! And Ethel Yeager flirting with every man who walks in."

"Who's Ethel Yeager?" I asked quickly, but Mama just looked like she wished she'd never brought it up.

"Never you mind that, Jens," she said, slapping food onto Roger's tray so fast that he looked up, his tiny eyebrows high with astonishment. "And Jim that's exactly what I mean. People think they can get anything they want at the auction. And I mean anything. It's not the place for decent people."

"Now, Greta, calm down. There's nothing that goes on at the auction that doesn't go on right out in the open every day. It's just a little more, well, concentrated there. A lot of it shoved into a small place. And people don't always get what they want there. A lot of them get what they need, though."

The auction was sounding more and more interesting to me, and I could hardly sit still. But Mama didn't say a word, just went on slamming food around the table. And Daddy looked cowed, just a little.

"And besides," he said, more softly, "I want to bid on that tractor Bobby Bates bought at Jack Franklin's foreclosure sale. He bought it from Jack for peanuts, and I know he's going to resell it tonight."

I could tell Daddy was now trying to get Mama's mind off the teasing he had done, but I knew it might be too late. Mama still looked all pursed up and mad. I knew things could go either way, and I held my breath, wanting to go so bad I could taste it.

"I'm warning you, Jim," Mama finally said, more calmly. "If you two aren't home by eleven you'd better not even let me hear the word 'auction' used in this house again!"

I nearly jumped up and down for joy right then and there.

On the eight-mile drive to the auction, Daddy talked about how Bobby Bates and his wife Carlene had started the Richards County Auction five years ago. They started it to fill a sad need. So many farmers were going broke and having to sell things from their farms and houses that the auctioneers in the area didn't have time enough to set up all the sales. So Bobby and Carlene opened the auction house and held a sale every Thursday night, and the farmers brought things to them to sell. Stuff like furniture and kitchen things and even farm machinery.

A few town people came out for it. But mostly people came from our neighborhood in the country—themselves farmers—needing cheap equipment to hang on.

Daddy also told me that the auction house was made from two long, skinny chicken houses hammered together. That's why I could expect to see a lot of feathers still floating around.

We got there just exactly in time for the auction to start. Bobby Bates was standing behind the long wooden-plank table in the far corner, and people were milling around in front of him. He spoke into a microphone hooked up around his shoulder to a powerpack. In his Stetson hat he had a red rhinestone pin shaped like a cowboy boot that kept flashing on and off, on and off.

"Friends, I'd appreciate it if you would get your numbers and gather up here," he said to the noisy crowd. "We'll be starting directly now."

Nobody seemed to be especially spurred into action by Bobby's announcement that he was about to start. They just kept milling around, talking and laughing. I could see a bench of old men by the big wood stove and I was pretty sure they were the ones that did the main spitting on the floor that Mama had talked about. They were all chewing hard as they could chew, anyway.

And there were several pretty ladies with big, bouncy hairdos and tight jeans, moving through the crowd like bright birds. I wondered which one of them was Ethel Yeager but knew better than to ask Daddy.

The place smelled like tobacco and hot dogs and the fields, and was brightly lit from bare bulbs hanging from the rafters. It was kind of like a big carnival, all in all. It gave you the same kind of feeling of being in a small bright place with a big stretch of quiet darkness just outside it on all sides.

"Jenser, go get us a couple of hot dogs and root beers, what you say?" Daddy gave me two dollars and pointed me toward the corner of the auction house where a big poster read CONCESSION STAND. I could see Bobby Bates's two fat daughters, Pam and Patricia, back behind the counter. They had on bright red *R. C. Auction House* T-shirts, stretched tight across their stomachs.

I began dodging through the crowd, saying hi to the people I recognized, which was about everybody but the city people, of course. At one point a peal of loud and wild laughter made everyone stop in their tracks and turn to face the old men on the bench. Something tiny and disgusting was squirming on the floor beneath a layer of brown ooze. My stomach gave a lurch, and I knew whatever it was down there, trapped beneath that chewing tobacco, it surely wished it was dead.

"Honestly, I wish to high heaven there was less spitting on my floor," Carlene Bates murmured to no one in particular, shaking her head as she hurried in their direction with a mop. The old men just laughed on, not noticing the look on her face.

When I finally reached the concession stand I had to wait. A lady and a man were leaning against the counter talking, and Pam and Patricia were leaning opposite them, listening. They showed no signs of wanting to wait on any other customers just at that moment. I didn't mind, because the first sentence I overheard the man say told me this lady was Ethel Yeager, and it sounded like this conversation might be lots more interesting than hot dogs and root beers.

"Well, Ethel, your boy has a good enough head on his shoulders," the man was saying. "I agree he's pretty young for marriage, but if they're in love, what you gonna do?"

Ethel Yeager threw her head back then and drained her root beer in one gulp. She had one hand stuck in the hip pocket of her jeans and she stuck her chest out, straining the buttons if you asked me. Her black curls fell in a shower down the back of her plaid shirt as she turned and laughed up at the man.

"Oh, Chuckie, I know what you say is right. I shouldn't take on so about my baby getting married. It's just that . . . well, do you picture me as an old grandmaw? Do you, baby?"

And then, still laughing, she took the man's arm and pulled him away from the counter, back toward the crowd of people milling around the tables of stuff to be sold. When he turned around I saw he was Charles Huffman, an old bachelor and one of our neighbors from down the road. Chuckie?! Mr. Huffman, with his thinning red hair and long, lean frame sure didn't look much like a "Chuckie" to me!

"Wow, isn't that romantic?" sighed Pam to her sister, as I edged to the counter and waited for them to notice me.

"What's so romantic about Ethel Yeager and Mr. Huffman?" I asked, tired of them not noticing me, even if they were in eighth grade.

"Not them, stupid! I mean Ethel's son, Ray Junior. It's so romantic the way he and Susan Potts ran off and got married last weekend."

Raymond Yeager and Susan Potts were married? And Raymond Yeager was Ethel's son? Raymond and Susan rode my bus and were only juniors in high school. Married? Wow!

"I'll have two hot dogs with the works and two root beers," I said, hoping I sounded like a person who came to this auction all the time and knew her way around.

"All right now, boys, let's do her," said Bobby Bates, and this time he picked up a rusty electric iron. Now that he had started, people seemed to believe he was going to start, and crowded around.

The bidding went slowly, through piles of old books and kitchen stuff and knickknacks. I got bored and began to wander through the building, looking at the bigger stuff to be bid later on.

In one corner there was a sign saying FURNITURE, and below it were two parts of a brown sectional sofa, an oak rocker with some slats missing from the back, and a gold footstool. This must have been a slow furniture night. The few pieces hunkered there in the shadows like a coyote pack.

In the other far corner of the room was the little John Deere tractor my father had come to bid on, the one that Bobby Bates had bought at Jack Franklin's foreclosure sale. I had heard Daddy say that Bobby had got the tractor so cheap it was more like stealing it, and tonight he would sell it for a good profit.

There was nothing much else to look at, just more tables of junky little stuff. I wandered back to the crowd and edged in to stand by my father.

"All right, boys and ladies, now I do recollect that you have been admiring my hat pin all evening," Bobby Bates was saying into his microphone. "Well, now is your chance to own one just like it, or to purchase one for your sweetheart. Who'll give five dollars for a hat pin?"

There was a little cardboard display set up on the table in front of Bobby, on which flashed a dozen tiny guitars, boots, and hearts bearing the tiny rhinestone words LOVER BOY.

"Well, I must say those are up to the minute, Bobby," an old lady, Mrs. Shroeder, said from the crowd. But nobody bid.

An explosion of laughter erupted from where the three old men sat by the stove, but everyone was used to it by now and no one bothered to turn around.

Bobby Bates was sweating, acting like he was dying to make a sale.

"I'll give fifty cents for one of them pins, Bobby," said a voice from way back in the crowd. I turned toward it and saw Jack Shire standing, hands deep in his overall pockets. "I would like to have a fancy guitar pin to wear when I go cruising in one of my convertibles."

Some people laughed quietly and shook their heads, but Bobby looked relieved and passed back the guitar pin.

Nobody else bought a pin, and Bobby finally gave up and moved on back to the old stuff that people had brought. I went to get another root beer to kill time, and sat down to drink it on the edge of one of the empty tables. I was getting really sleepy and was glad they were almost to the furniture. After that would come the tractor—then we could go home.

Finally, they got to the end of the last long table of what I had started thinking of as junk, and moved on to the furniture corner. I could see the three old men on their bench were asleep. I slid down off the table, my legs tingly from sitting so long, and went to find Daddy and stand beside him.

Bobby Bates was standing behind the two pieces of the sectional sofa, one hand on the back of each piece.

"All right now, ladies, I want you to looky here at this fine sofa. You can see this has not hardly seen much wear at all. This and a TV set would make you a room."

"I'll go fifteen dollars," said Mrs. Shroeder, firmly.

"Sixteen," said another voice from the crowd, which I thought belonged to one of the teachers at the school, Mrs. Crowder.

"I have sixteen, sixteen. Do I hear seventeen?"

"Seventeen," said Ethel Yeager.

Several people gasped, and began to whisper. The bidding hadn't been fast and furious like this all night. It was waking people up from the dozey state they'd been drifting around in for hours.

"All right! Can I have eighteen now?" asked Bobby Bates, his voice tight and hopeful.

"Bobby, I say twenty dollars for that set," said Ethel, shaking back her black curls and standing with one hip stuck out, the other leg bent forward at the knee.

The crowd gasped, and Bobby wiped sweat from his face.

"Do I hear twenty-one?" he asked. "Twenty-one?"

No one else spoke. You could tell Bobby was eager to end the bidding before any of the bidders came to their senses and realized how much they'd agreed to pay.

"Sold, then, to Ethel Yeager!"

The crowd, frozen throughout the bidding, breathed again. Then someone started up the John Deere, and the smell of diesel fuel was strong in the room. The crowd walked away, toward the little tractor, the last thing to be bid. Only Ethel Yeager and Charlie Huffman were left to poke and prod the sofa Ethel had just bought. Charlie was pointing out a big hole in the seat when I walked by.

Daddy was standing close to the tractor with several other men, and you could see from the expressions on their faces they were anxious to bid on it.

"Now, boys, this here's what you've been waiting for all night, a bunch of you, I reckon," Bobby was saying. "Ain't she a beauty? Well took care of, every man here can see that. Who'll start the bidding?"

And then, Jack Franklin stepped from the shadows where he had been standing with his wife, Mary, all night. The other men seemed to part for him, letting him step up to the tractor he had once owned and lost at his sale last fall. He ran his hands over the sides, stopped to look slowly underneath the engine cover.

"I say, boys, who's got a bid for me?" asked Bobby again, his eyes glued to Jack where he was bent, inspecting his old tractor.

Jack Franklin straightened slowly up then, and stood in the center of the circle of men, beside the John Deere. The other men dropped their eyes as Bobby and Jack faced each other silently.

"All right, Jack," Bobby said quietly. "Have you got the $500 dollars I paid for her?"

My father and the other men began to drift silently back into the crowd, as Bobby and Jack shook hands. Then Mary came forward and took Jack's arm, and everybody else began gathering up the things they'd bought.

The auction was over for another week.

7 *The Earth Begins to Move Beneath My Feet*

In the truck on the way home, neither of us said anything for a long time. I was so sleepy I could hardly keep my eyes open, and everything I had heard and seen spun in a circle in my mind as I stared out my window at the stars.

"Well, what'd you think, Jens?" Daddy finally asked, as we turned off the wide road and onto one of the gravel roads past Iola.

I shrugged. "I think it's a shame you didn't get the tractor, after waiting so long and everything. It just doesn't seem fair that nobody got to bid on it."

Daddy didn't say anything, and we moved along through the night for a mile or so. Then his deep, comfortable voice filled the dark cab of the truck.

"Jens, I don't always have the words to tell you things," he said slowly. "But I'd like for you to take my word for it when I tell you that fairness is more complicated than it sometimes seems. What I mean is, you mustn't let 'fair' control your life, understand me?"

No, I didn't. Not then, anyway, though I do more now. I think.

"But Daddy, you told me yourself in the car that you would bid up to $900 for that tractor! And yet Jack Franklin got it for just $500, and nobody even said 'boo!' "

Again, Daddy was quiet for a while before speaking.

"Jens, last fall the bank foreclosed on Jack and Mary and sold their 450 acres, all their machinery, and most everything they had to show for thirty-five years of farming. They sold it all in one afternoon, leaving them with the house and forty acres. And in the months since, no one has seen much of the Franklins. They've stayed at home, away from folks in Iola. I believe they've been too ashamed—and too hurt—to come back out into the world. When Jack finally showed himself tonight and wanted to buy back the tractor that was sold out from under him last fall, well, then folks knew they were ready to start their lives up again, and it was the place of the rest of us to help them do it. Jack will use that little John Deere, I reckon, to farm that forty acres he has left. Bobby charged him what he paid for it. He could have got more, sure. One of us could have got a bargain too. But it wasn't right that we do that, Jens. We have to give up on fair sometimes. But without right, we'd be nowhere."

This was quite a speech for my silent father, the longest one by far I'd ever heard him make. I swallowed hard, looking back out my window at the faraway line the hills made against the black-violet sky. I wanted to ask him now about the thing I'd heard him say the night Brenda Miller's father died, the thing about the land swallowing all of us. But I couldn't get up the nerve. Instead, I told him something else strange.

"I know who Ethel Yeager is now. She's mad at her son for running off and getting married, but still she got him that furniture tonight. Boy, I wouldn't have done it."

He smiled, and reached over to pull my hair.

"You wouldn't have, huh? Hey, you better not tell your mother you were snooping around, trying to find out who Ethel Yeager was."

With anybody else I would have said that I wasn't snooping, but Daddy knew me too well for me to have to.

"And another thing," I went on. "Those old men are gross! Spitting on the floor! Gross!"

My father pulled the pickup into our long, dusty driveway. The kitchen light was on, and the upstairs bathroom light. I saw the clock on the dashboard read 11:50, which might have been either fast or slow about fifteen minutes because that clock's never right. Still, we were late, and I wondered if Daddy was afraid of what Mama would say.

"I wouldn't strictly say they were just spitting on the floor, Jens," he said, calmly. I decided he wasn't afraid. "I'd say those old men are spitting at spiders, and maybe an occasional grasshopper. Makes them feel powerful, is my guess."

And walking back to the house, with the early spring dew set already and soaking our feet, I squished my toes and remembered what Daddy had said that night at the dinner table, that people don't always get what they want at the auction, but a lot of them get what they need.

And I guessed those old men needed to feel powerful, and that Jack Franklin needed his tractor. And Ethel Yeager might not have wanted to be a grandma, but deep inside I guessed she needed her son to get that furniture.

On the bus the next morning I told Marla we were losing our herd.

"Oh, Jens! No! When?"

"A government man is coming to get them, probably tomorrow."

Her brown eyes looked deep with sympathy.

She's a good friend, no matter what. I got a lump in my throat at her reaction and forgot about the earlier plan I had made to play it cool and act like it was no big deal.

"When I helped Daddy milk this morning it was all I could do to look at the cows," I told her quietly. "I just feel so guilty somehow. And scared. Things are changing, Marla. Have you noticed? People losing their farms right and left. Who knows, maybe we're next."

She shivered and hunched up her shoulders.

"Don't talk like that, Jens. Everything will be all right. You'll see."

Then she thumbed through her math book, and I could tell she was thinking.

"Hey, I've got an idea," she said suddenly, slamming the book shut and looking toward me with excitement. "Spend the night with me next Friday, and I'll get my mother to take us into Crestville on Saturday! That'll get your mind off—you know—losing your herd."

Her voice faded away at the end, like she was sorry she had brought the herd up again. But her plan sounded great. We only got to go shopping in Crestville a few times a year, and it was always a lot of fun to eat out at a drive-in and try on clothes in the department stores.

"Wow, if your mom would take us, that would be great," I told her, feeling that maybe she was right, maybe things would work out and I was only imagining the fear I felt. After all, when you thought about it, it was silly to think things would ever change. They had gone on the same way too long.

We got off the bus and were hurrying for class when John Frank came running up behind us. I held my lunch sack closer to me, shielding my banana and turning to throw an insult in his direction. But he went to Marla's side, ignoring me.

"Hey, wait up! What's a guy have to do to get to walk you to class?" he asked her.

I dropped back, and when I was a few feet behind them I hurried around a corner and leaned against the door to the boiler room, breathing hard and trying not to cry.

To think that only seconds ago I had felt happy, had been sure things would be all right and would never change! Well, that just showed what a jerk I was. Things were changing everywhere around me. The ground was moving beneath my feet like in an earthquake, and I couldn't find a safe place to stand.

"Jennifer, are you, uh, all right?"

I looked up and quit pushing on my teeth long enough to see Arthur Boatright looking around the corner at me. He held his books loosely in one hand, and held his jacket, slung over his shoulder, with the other. He was so tall that he blocked out the sunlight coming in a glare from the big windows across the hall, and made me feel flustered, there in the shadows, alone.

"Uh, yes. Yes. I'm okay."

I smiled and nodded my head up and down too quickly, like a silly rag doll or something.

"Sure? Maybe I could, well, walk you where you're going or something."

And in that second all thoughts of the herd and Marla and my misery went out of my head. And something new came flooding in. I can't exactly explain it, but all of a sudden I kind of understood that it wasn't just this spring that it would feel like the earth was moving under me. It was, probably, all my life from now on out. But maybe there would be new things in the picture, things I hadn't counted on or even thought about to help me find my balance.

Arthur Boatright stood there solid and strong, and unbelievable as it sounds, every bit of his attention was focused right smack dab on me.

I kind of floated through the rest of that day, aware that my neck was burning and that most of the reason for that was that Arthur was sitting three rows behind me in class. When it was finally time to go home, I didn't have the nerve to look over my shoulder at him, but when Marla and I were in our seat on the bus, I glanced in his direction, and he smiled at me.

"Know what, Marla?" I whispered to her, "it's

kind of late this year, with less than two weeks of school left and all. But if when we're in seventh grade, you want to sit with John Frank part of the time on the bus, well, I mean, I would think that was all right."

Marla looked surprised, then looked over her shoulder to where Arthur still smiled toward me.

"Well, that's big of you, Jens," she said, then broke down in giggles.

That next Friday night, when I spent the night at Marla's, was the last time I can remember feeling really lighthearted and happy.

We lay in her twin beds after her mother made us turn off the light, hugging our feather pillows and calling them John Frank and Arthur until we were exhausted from laughing so much. Then we went and sat on the carpet under Marla's big bay window and looked out sleepily across the fields.

"It's warm enough to have the windows open at night," she whispered, and we both hopped up and pushed the screens and windows of her room open. It got chilly, then cold, but we dragged the blankets off her bed and sat by the open bay window anyway.

"Do you realize," she said, her breath a frosty cloud, "that there's absolutely nothing separating us from the stars and other planets?"

"Well, there's ozone and all that stuff," I answered, blowing on my hands. "So it's not exactly nothing."

But I knew what she meant. She was talking about the same kind of thing I always felt in the milk shed, looking at the wishing star. If you could jump hard enough, nothing could stop you from going as high as high could be. Anything was possible.

"Anything's possible," Marla said dreamily.

"As you always say," I reminded her, smiling under the blanket that I'd pulled over my nose.

She smiled back, but didn't answer, just sat looking out at the night, up at the stars. I watched her, and thought as I so often did how I ought to be jealous of her. She was so perfect looking, so sweet, had such a great house.

"Marla, do you think we're going to lose our farm? Honestly."

I don't know where the question came from. It must have been boiling inside of me for a while, and pushing it out made my chest ache.

She turned to me with a jerk and threw aside her blanket to come and put an arm around my shoulders.

"Oh, Jens, no! Of course not! Your mother was born on that farm, and your dad's lived around here forever. Things like that just don't happen."

Of course, I knew they did, and so did she. The ache in my chest moved to my throat and throbbed there. And the stars looked so bright that I wanted to jump up and tear them out of the sky with anger.

"Maybe not, Marla," I finally forced out through chattering teeth. From the cold, or from fear? Probably a little of both. "Maybe not, but anything's possible. Even bad things."

The next morning, right after breakfast, Marla's mother drove us to Crestville. We took their pickup with the stock racks up, the back full of feeder pigs that Mrs. Stevens needed to drop off at the livestock market.

When we were younger, Marla and I thought it was kind of fun going to the livestock market in Crestville, riding in the front of a pickup full of swaying animals.

But now we thought it was awful. After all, what could be more embarrassing than stopping at a hamburger place and going inside, then coming back out to find that nobody would park within three spaces of the smelly contraption you were riding in?

"You're being too sensitive," Mrs. Stevens said when Marla pointed this out to her, trying to get her to take the car instead and make Mr. Stevens take the pigs in later. "Probably because you're grouchy from whispering all night in a freezing cold room."

How did she know? Really, how do mothers find out stuff like that?

And so we took the truck, and Marla and I rode in stony silence, punishing Mrs. Stevens. She let us off downtown and went on to the market.

"Now remember, girls, stay right on the square. And I'll meet you at Bentley's in an hour."

Marla nodded shortly from the sidewalk, her face pink, looking out of the corner of her eyes and hoping nobody we knew had seen us get out of the truck.

"Come on, let's go look at Colland's for clothes," I said to her, grabbing her sleeve as the pickup finally pulled from the curb and left us on our own. A feeling of freedom and adventure was welling up in me, and I knew Marla felt it too. This was practically the first time we'd been on our own in the city.

We worked our way around the square from Colland's, looking at clothes and getting those great malted milk balls in white sacks from Winthrop's Pharmacy.

"Don't crunch them, suck them," Marla told me. "They last longer."

I'd tried that before, but it made the roof of my mouth sore. I was starting to tell her this when I happened to look in the window of Douglas's Hardware Store, and my words froze in my mouth.

I could feel the sweet chocolate dribbling down my throat, but I couldn't even seem to swallow. All I could do was stare.

"Jens?" Marla followed my gaze through the big plate glass window to where Mr. Douglas was talking and laughing with a man, shaking his hand.

"Your father," she breathed. "What's he doing in Crestville?"

I didn't answer, just walked to the door of the hardware store and pushed my shoulder against it. And then I was inside with Marla close behind me, staring at my father. He turned around, looking surprised. He was dressed up, like for church, and the top of his forehead looked white where he always wore his Corn Producers hat and didn't get tan.

"Jens? Say, I'd forgotten you said you were coming to town today," he said, looking funny, kind of flustered or something.

"Daddy? Why aren't you in the field, planting?"

And then it dawned on me, and relief flooded through me that made my knees feel weak. Something must have broken on the combine, some part that Daddy needed to bring to town to get replaced! Why had I felt so worried when I saw him?

I laughed and hugged him, there in the middle of the store and everything.

"I'm sorry, Daddy," I said into his corduroy jacket. "I just figured out that you needed a part or something. I wish I'd known so I could have picked it up for you. I know how you hate to waste field time in the spring."

I felt his rough, solid hand squeezing my shoulder, but he didn't speak. Instead, I heard the voice of Mr. Douglas, the owner of the hardware store, but after his first few words his voice sounded far away.

"Sweetheart, your father here is too smart to stay in a dead-end racket like farming," he laughed. "Come Monday, he starts working here for me."

8 *Mama*

"Shall we stop at Burger Heaven for some lunch?" Mrs. Stevens asked softly as we drove out of Crestville. I didn't say anything, just kept staring down at my hands, but Marla looked across me at her mother and shook her head. Mrs. Stevens reached over and patted my knee, looking puzzled.

I hadn't made a scene in the hardware store, and I was proud of that. I wasn't a baby, after all, and I knew that Daddy needed for me to keep things inside me and act like nothing horrible had happened. I could do that, for a while. But I wished and wished again that Mrs. Stevens would drive faster so I could get home. I needed the clover field, or the milk shed, or something.

When we pulled into our driveway, there was a blue car there that I didn't recognize. Marla got out first and stood holding the truck door open for me. When I slid out, she took my arm.

"Jens, I . . . I don't think you should jump to conclusions yet. I mean, just because your father is going to be working in town now, doesn't mean you're going to be leaving, you know."

I tried to be nice and smile but when I pulled my arm away I couldn't help jerking it and I couldn't meet her eyes, either. After all, what could she ever know about it? Everything in her life was perfect. She wasn't the one about to lose everything she'd ever loved.

I stumbled toward the house, tears blinding me now that I could finally let them out, and shoved open the kitchen door. My mother was sitting at the round oak kitchen table, with two men in suits across from her. There were a bunch of papers on the table. She stood up quickly, gripping the back of her chair, and I saw the knuckles of her long, delicate fingers were white.

"Jens, I thought you were spending the whole day with Marla," she said, her voice strained and anxious. "I . . . I didn't expect you home till much later."

I looked hard at the two uncomfortable-looking men in the shadowy room and then I remembered where I had seen the long, fancy blue car before. I had seen it parked outside the bank. These were bank men, here to talk about taking our farm!

I ran up the stairs, slammed into my room and

locked the door behind me. I wanted to cry and cry but I was too mad.

I was mad at the bank men for bringing those awful papers and spreading them out on the table that had belonged to my great-grandmother like they owned the place or something. I was mad at Marla for being so perfect and having John Frank, and I wouldn't be here now to have Arthur. I was mad at Roger for being a baby who didn't have to understand all this and could just be happy and everything.

But as I paced through that room where I'd lived all my life, looked out the window across the fields that had been plowed by my family for generations, I quickly decided who I was the most mad at. She stood at the center of this like the core of a rotten apple.

My mother. She had never loved this place like my father and I did. She had never felt it inside her, her whole life and spirit and soul. She had probably even wanted this to happen, so that she could live in the city where her prettiness would be seen by lots of people. Where she wouldn't have to work her delicate hands so raw. Where she could show off adorable, perfect little Roger to her neighbors.

I watched, shaking all over, as my mother walked the men to their car, and turned, her head down, to walk slowly back inside. Then I ran from my room to meet her.

"You never liked this place," I spat at her from the stairs. "Well, are you satisfied now? Now that you've ruined Daddy's life and mine?"

I couldn't believe that I was talking to her like this. But then, I didn't feel real, had never been nearly this upset. I felt ages and ages older than I had been a month before. I felt lost and alone, without a map, so what did it matter what I said or did?

Her hands flew to the sides of her face and she shook her head. "Jens, don't," she whispered. "Please, we're all very upset. But don't make it worse. You just can't understand."

"We're losing the farm, aren't we? I can understand that," I practically yelled at her.

She dropped her eyes and grabbed the back of a chair, slumping against it. "Yes, Jennifer. It looks like we probably are."

Everything inside me turned to ice. Before there had been hot pain, but the certainty of what was coming froze all that. I wasn't real now. Like I'd suspected, nothing mattered anymore.

"Then I hate you!" I screamed at her. And then the tears came so fast I nearly lost my balance as I raced down the stairs and out the house, slamming the kitchen door as hard as I could.

I'd woken Roger. I heard him crying as I ran to the barn and got my bike. I pictured my mother going, upset herself, to comfort him, and felt a pang of shame.

"But too bad for her. He's the only one she loves, so let her have him," I sobbed to myself. Then I sped dizzily on down the road to Iola, not knowing what I would do there, only knowing I had to get away from home.

By the time I reached the edge of town, my head was splitting and my legs ached from the fury that had gone into my peddling. I had some vague plan to go on through town, out the highway and on to wherever it led me. After all, what did anyone care back home about me? Well, maybe my father cared, but he wouldn't be around enough from now on for that to matter. He'd still have adorable little Roger, anyway, to occupy what little time at home he had.

I felt fresh tears crowd my chest, but before I could let them out, somebody else's sobs shocked me into swallowing them, and I stopped to listen, both feet flat on the asphalt.

"Who's there?" I croaked out, my throat dry.

The sounds of crying—raspy and hard—came from the ditch by the side of the road. I put a hand over my eyes to block the sun and searched among the tangled dewberry vines. I saw the bright orange thongs first, then followed them upward to the pale legs and long, wrinkled skirt of Betty. She was sitting in the shadows of the long weeds beside the road, tears mixing into mud with the dirt on her face.

"Pay me no mind," she said, when she saw me watching her, "and leave me be."

"Betty? Hey, it's just me, Jens. Are you . . . okay?"

Before I could dodge or even tell what was happening, I was hit in the left shoulder and side of the face with a handful of dark, squashy fruit—dewberries.

"I tell you, leave me be, Jens!" Betty yelled, hiccuping from the ditch where she crouched, ready to sling another handful of berries. "All you high and mighty people can just leave me be! You took my Petey, now you can just get back, because I'll kill you if'n you come close!"

I looked on both sides of the road and over my shoulder. Sure enough, there was no Petey anywhere. I'd never seen Betty without Petey in whistling distance.

I knew then something was awfully wrong. And a funny thing occurred to me. Always before I had been a little afraid of Betty, avoided her because of the scary poorness that seemed attached to her. But today, I could see that wasn't a part of her at all, any more than losing the farm was a part of me. There was no shame to Betty's situation, though some folks seemed to look at it that way. Sadness, but no shame. She was just a kid, like me, with thoughts and hopes and fears.

I pushed my bike to the edge of the road and climbed into the ditch beside her.

"Don't hit me with those, Betty, okay? I won't bother you. I just want to know about Petey. Is he okay?"

She looked at the handful of berries she held, her long blonde hair sweaty against her neck. Then she squeezed, hard, and the berry juice ran down her arm, onto her skirt. She was shaking all over.

"Petey got the pneumonia," she said, so low I hardly heard. "They come took him to the hospital, the county people did. They say if he makes it, he'll go to a foster home, more'n likely."

I sat shocked, staring at her hand, hearing the sound of Petey's sad, rusted wagon in my mind.

"Oh, Betty, that's awful. But why did your mama let them take him?" I finally asked. "She could have put him in the hospital herself. The state would have paid, wouldn't they?"

Betty still stared at her hand. "Mama done left weeks ago," she said, dully. "I don't know where she went. She give Petey to me."

And then she took her eyes from the berries and turned them on me.

And when I saw the panic and fear in them I realized she wasn't a bunch older than me, like I'd always thought. She was just about my age, maybe fourteen at the most, but no more. The only real difference in us was that I had a real family, people to care about me, and she didn't. I had a mother.

"I love Petey," she said. "Understand, Jens?"

"Yeah. I have a brother too, you know," I whispered. And until that moment I don't think I'd ever stopped to think how much I loved fat, funny Roger.

"And you won't tell no one where I'm at? I mean to hide here, eat berries till I make a plan to get Petey back. Mama, she give Petey to me."

I nodded, but I wanted so bad to ask who she'd given Betty to. Of course I knew the awful answer. Nobody. Betty belonged to nobody right now.

I stood up and felt the scratchy vines tearing at my jeans. Looking down, I saw Betty's bare legs crisscrossed with tiny red lines, her filthy feet torn and bruised in her sandals from the gravel roads where she mostly lived.

I climbed out of the ditch and pulled splinters and burrs from my jeans, then picked up my bike and leaned hard on the handlebars as I pushed off my Nikes against the pedals.

"Here, Betty," I said, throwing my shoes toward her, then hurrying to turn my bike and point it back toward home, "could be these will fit you."

I had the miles home to think and practice but still I was queasy with dread as I passed the mulberry tree and saw the farm ahead. Had I actually told Mama I hated her?

I stood for a long time outside the house, collecting my dignity. I'd decided the best thing to do was to go in with my chin high and to calmly explain to my mother that I was sorry for what I'd said, and that it wouldn't happen again.

I climbed the four porch stairs, pushed open the squeaky screen door. I could tell from the quietness in the house that Roger was finishing the nap I'd woken him from before. Mama sat slumped at the kitchen table, her head on her arms folded in front of her. When she heard me come in, she sat up, startled. Maybe she'd been sleeping. Her face was pale and drawn, her beautiful eyes lined with black circles.

"Jens . . ." she whispered, turning to me, half rising.

My throat filled up and I started to tremble.

"Oh, Mama, what's the matter with me?" I sobbed, running toward her, dropping to my knees beside her and putting my head in her lap.

Well, so much for dignity, which I guess you ought to have some of when you're almost thirteen.

But I suddenly didn't feel almost thirteen. As Mama stroked my hair and let me cry in her lap that afternoon, I felt like a baby again. And for that few minutes, it felt pretty good.

*   *   *

"Jens? Let's go for a walk, while Roger is still asleep."

I raised my head and looked up at her. The tears had mostly dried on my face by then, and it felt stiff, partly from the dewberry juice where Betty had clobbered me. My legs were asleep from kneeling like that, and my hair was soggy from sweat and tears. But I felt a million times better.

I got up and the two of us left the kitchen and walked toward the clover field.

"You know," she told me after a while of walking in silence, "you were right, in a way. Even though I was born here, leaving this place won't hurt me the way it will hurt your father, and the way it will hurt you. I know that's so, though I don't know why it is. It just seems to me that some people are born to the land, born with a need to feel its cycles, to be a part of its joys and disappointments. You and your father are like that, but when we go I'll mostly just miss the memories. Back in high school, when some girl or other would move to the city, I remember I always felt a pang of envy. I used to imagine the lights, the bustle. Sometimes I'd cry myself to sleep imagining."

We sat down in the clover, near enough the house to hear if Roger woke. I picked a long purple stalk and chewed on it, kind of shocked. It was the first time I'd ever heard my mother talk about her own feelings when she was a girl. I guess I didn't realize mothers ever had dreams, or hopes.

"Mama, when you were my age, did you have everything figured out, or did it seem like each day just scrambled things around more and more?"

She smiled. "Honey, I think the world is too beautiful and too sad at the same time to ever figure out. And I imagine things are more confusing for you than they were for me at your age. You're like your dad, sensitive and always asking hard questions."

My heart was pounding. She had called me sensitive. That was a nice word, wasn't it, like you'd use to compliment somebody with? And surely she meant it as a compliment when she said I was like Daddy, because she loved Daddy. Was it possible she really did like me after all, even if I wasn't cute and little and easygoing like Roger? Not like me because she was stuck with me, but really like me?

I decided to try a test to see if I had it wrong.

"Sorry," I said quietly, "I wish I'd turned out to be the kind of daughter you wanted."

It worked—even better than I'd hoped. She drew in her breath real quick and took my arms in her hands and turned me to face her, frowning.

"Oh, Jens, I've been proud of you every day of your life! Don't you honestly know that?"

"I don't know," I whispered, not meeting her

eyes. Suddenly I could hardly talk. "It just always seems like you're so pretty and quiet and perfect, kind of like Marla. I can never be like you. Roger's like you, even if he is a boy."

And then a funny thing happened. Mama started crying, something I'd only seen her do when somebody died. She kept holding my arms, but her shoulders started hunching up and down and she dropped her head. I could tell she was really shaken up by the sound of her voice.

"Oh, Jennifer, I did everything I could think of to keep us from losing this farm. And I did it for you more than for anyone because I know what it means to you. Can't you believe that? Can't you believe that I love you that much?"

"Mama, I'm sorry I said I hated you," I choked, leaning forward and hugging her.

She hugged me back, and we stayed like that for a while, with the clover bobbing all around us. Then Roger squealed from the kitchen.

"Jens, I know you don't hate me," Mama whispered, pulling away and smiling through her tears as she held my face in her hands for a few seconds before getting up and going to see about Roger.

See? Nice people like Mama and Marla always just know those things, but it seems like I have to learn them over and over again, the hard way.

*   *   *

When I got back inside I hunted through the junk on my closet floor until I found the pair of bluejeans with the torn, bloody knee I'd been wearing when I made the list of worries under the mulberry tree.

I read them back over:

(1) my horrible teeth
(2) losing the herd
(3) John Frank being so nice to Marla
(4) what Daddy said about the land eating us
(5) Mama not liking me very well

With a green Magic Marker I crossed out numbers 3 and 5. I thought about adding a number 6, but losing the farm seemed more like a big final deal than just a worry.

9 *The Surprise Party*

The next weeks went by in a jumbled up rush, and I had trouble getting my bearings.

To begin with, Daddy started working long hours at the store in Crestville, and I hardly saw him. When he was home he didn't talk much, just acted real worn out. I'd seen him spend twenty hours out in the fields, and he didn't look half as tired when he came in as he looked now after ten hours in town. Mama usually sent me up to bed soon as I'd told him about my day, and then I would hear their voices, droning on and on, in the kitchen. That was a strange, scary sound. No laughter, no radio music in the background. Just that droning on and on.

A few times they went to the bank together, and those days Daddy went to work late. But they always came home looking even more exhausted than when they left, so I knew better than to ask if the bank men had changed their minds.

Mama began dragging things out of drawers and cabinets, sorting and boxing. Once when I came home from school there were three big empty cardboard boxes on the stairs.

"Jens? Why don't you take those boxes to your room to see if you can, you know, pack a few things up," Mama said softly from where she was sorting greens at the sink.

I swallowed hard and edged past the boxes, on up the stairs. I just couldn't do it. I had the strong feeling that once I started packing things up, all of this would be real. That was the same reason I didn't ask where we were going, and when we were going there. I didn't want to know because it would have been admitting that things were over.

I spent a lot of time in the milk shed and the clover field, trying to memorize every detail, every blossom and every star.

And I started wondering about things. Like, would I still feel the cycles of the land when we lived in town? Would I know from the smell of the air when it was time to plant and when harvest was only a week away? Would I be able to eat storebought eggs? I couldn't eat them now, but Mama always said I was just too persnickety.

Even Roger seemed sad. Or maybe upset is more

like it. He had never been whiney, but now nothing would satisfy him. Mama borrowed my aunt's bicycle child seat—the one she'd used when my cousins were little—and fastened it on the back of my bike. I started taking Roger for long rides, which was the one surefire way to get him out of a gripey mood. We rode my bike together that way for miles, Roger flapping his fat arms and laughing that open-mouthed laugh of his.

Then toward the end of May, school was over for the summer, and the heat set in. The cows were long gone, and we weren't planting a garden for the first time ever. I spent the days wandering around, trying to memorize things. I felt lost unless I had Roger with me, which really helped.

Then came the day we killed the chickens.

"I know this won't be easy for you, Jens, but I need your help," Mama told me the day before, taking my shoulders in her hands like she had been a lot lately. "We're down to just eleven in the flock, so if we start at dawn tomorrow we can have them all in the freezer by afternoon."

I watched her that next morning as, one by one, she stuck their scrawny necks into the slot in the old elm stump and whacked their heads off with the ax. It amazed me that she could do that, delicate as she was. But then, in the past days I'd seen that she could do a lot of things I wouldn't have thought she could.

When she had their heads off and they'd quit flopping around, I picked them up by the feet and dunked them in the pots of boiling water we had over the fire in the side yard. Then I started picking out feathers until I was so covered with them I felt like a big white chicken myself. When she finished the axing she took the bare chickens from me and cut out their insides with her sharpest knife, a job she showed me how to do so I could help when I'd finished the feathers.

I'd thought I'd cry clear through the whole thing, but it was so interesting I forgot to. Roger thought it was scary at first but soon changed his mind and found it hilarious.

"Boo, Rogie! I'm a big fat chicken snowman!" I said, rushing toward him with my feather-covered arms out. He howled with laughter until he started hiccuping.

I'm glad I'd never gotten around to naming the chickens. I think that was why they were easier to lose than the cows.

Three Thursdays in a row Daddy took a pickup load of stuff to the Richards County Auction. I tried not to pay attention to what he was taking. It was mostly barn stuff, but one night I couldn't stop myself from looking out the window as he was pulling down the driveway, and I saw my mother's little sewing rocking chair balanced beside a bunch of chains and barrels and stuff in the truck bed.

"Mama!" I called, running down the stairs and into the kitchen. "Daddy accidentally took your rocker, the one with the embroidered seat! Should I run out and stop him?"

She went on peeling potatoes without turning around from the sink. "No, Jens, that's all right. I told him to," she said quietly and evenly.

"But Mama, that was Grandma's chair! You said it was real old—an antique!"

She slowly put down her knife and rinsed the potato in her hand, then wiped her hands on her apron and turned around to face me. I'd gotten used to the dark circles around her eyes the past weeks, but she was so thin now that it came as a shock to me to see her cheekbones so sharp in the shadowy light.

"Jennifer, stop and think for a minute. In a few weeks we'll be setting up house in a completely different place. We have a lot of expenses coming up, and no real income for a while, except the few dollars your father makes in town. We need every penny we can scratch together."

I stood shaking my head. "But . . . but Grandma's chair . . ." I said helplessly. For the first time, it hit me that we were really poor now, and that our future was uncertain. It was something I hadn't imagined could happen to us. Losing the farm was horrible enough, but I hadn't felt the second wave of awfulness until that moment. The first wave was sadness, the second was more like shame.

"Mama, what's going to happen to us?" I asked her, my throat tight.

And though she held out her arms and I let her hug me, she felt all boney and fragile, not really solid and comforting at all.

I realized then that she didn't have any answers, just a mindful of hard questions—a lot like mine.

I can't exactly explain why but I avoided Marla and my other friends more and more, beginning with the day we came home from seeing my dad in Crestville and found the bank car in our driveway. I felt real funny around them, though they kept calling and trying to get me to do things with them. I just couldn't be like my old self, laughing and worrying about all kinds of little stuff. Not now. And anyway, since that day I saw Betty crying in the ditch I had sort of understood that there's no disgrace to being poor, but understanding and feeling are two different things. I felt ashamed.

Besides, why bother? They wouldn't be my friends much longer. Sometimes it was a relief to think about that, to know we would be making a new start somewhere where people wouldn't feel sorry for us. But usually my head ached and my chest felt tight when I thought about it.

Especially when I thought about losing Marla.

One humid afternoon late in June I was in the clover field when I saw Mama come out the kitchen door and start toward me. I was surprised and quickly opened the book I'd brought with me.

"I need to run over to Marge Stevens's house for a minute," she said, pushing her black hair from her eyes as the wind caught it. "You come with me."

"Can't. I'm too busy reading," I mumbled.

She put her hands on her hips. "Reading, or moping?"

"Reading, of course," I said, staring harder than ever at the page in front of me. "I don't mope."

She nodded thoughtfully as I watched her out the corner of my eyes, wishing she'd go back inside and leave me with my thoughts. But she only reached down and grabbed my wrist.

"Come on, it'll be good for you to be with Marla again. Marge says she thinks you're mad at her, since you never return her phone calls."

"Since when is it a federal crime to be busy around here?" I exploded, slamming shut my book.

But I knew the difference between Mama's asking and her insisting, so I got to my feet and followed her back to the house.

When we drove up in front of Marla's house, there were a bunch of bikes in the grass by the driveway, which seemed a little funny to me. I didn't have time to try to figure it out, though, because Mama was walking quickly toward the front door, smiling back at me and gesturing for me to hurry. I really got suspicious then that something was up. She was grinning ear to ear, almost giggling.

She knocked on the door, and Mrs. Stevens answered it, wearing the same kind of expression, like she knew a funny secret or something. And then about a million kids pulled the door open wide and jumped up and down yelling "Surprise! Surprise!," and Mama pushed me inside the house, into the middle of all that yelling and laughing.

"What's going on?" I whispered. I really didn't know.

"It's a surprise party, silly!" Shelley cried, jumping up and down. "We worked a whole week on it and did all the decorating and everything!"

And I guess I knew they were all waiting for me to act all excited and happy and everything, but instead I could only stand there frozen. Because suddenly my mind was filled with a picture of the day we'd given Brenda Miller the chalk and card and jelly beans. I was seeing how we had all charged up to her, so pleased with ourselves, but how Brenda's eyes were filled with a sadness we couldn't have any idea about. And I felt in the pit of my stomach how she had felt then, on the outside of the planning and the feeling good, looking sadly in.

"Why?" I asked, my eyes filled with angry, frustrated tears.

"Why what, Jens?" Marla had stepped from the crowd of kids to come close beside me. Everybody was getting quiet, their laughter fading, acting like they didn't know what to do.

I looked around the big fancy living room of Marla's house, took in all the crepe paper streamers and bright colored balloons. I saw the table of punch and a cake with a smiley face on it, just like we'd put on Brenda's card when we didn't know what to say.

"Why are you humiliating me like this?" I whispered to her, then turned and ran out the door. I vaguely saw Mrs. Stevens's worried face as I rushed by.

Marla followed me. Halfway to the gravel road she caught up and grabbed me roughly by the left arm, just above my elbow. That was probably the biggest shock of my life, being grabbed like that by sweet, gentle little Marla.

"Don't you know how hard this is for your

friends?" she yelled, as she tried to force me to stop. "What do you expect, for us to be geniuses or something? For us to know what to say and what to do? Well, we don't know how to treat you, Jens! You won't talk to us!"

"Of course you don't know, with your perfect looks and your perfect house and everything!" I was fuming now. "It makes all of you feel better to plan a party like this, but what about me, huh? What about me? None of this is fair! It's not fair at all!"

Marla let go of my arm and dropped her head.

"I know," she said quietly. "I'm sorry. We just wanted you to know we care."

My anger was cooling now, and I was starting to breathe normally again. I was suddenly aware of what a fool I'd just made of myself in front of practically everybody in the world. I rubbed my arm.

"Wow, I can't believe you actually grabbed me like that," I said sheepishly.

"Yeah, me either." She looked pleased with herself. "So maybe I won't always be such a wimp, huh?"

"You're no wimp," I said quietly. "And thanks for the party."

"Will you come back to it?"

"After acting like such a jerk? Anyway, I don't know what to say to people these days. I feel all mixed up, embarrassed and everything."

I remembered, then. That's what we hadn't known about Brenda. That she was mixed up and embarrassed. Her sadness made us feel useless and clumsy, but we did really want to make her smile again.

"You know everybody understands," Marla said softly. "We just want you to not be so sad, that's all."

Everybody was quiet and flustered when we walked back inside, but that didn't last long once they saw we were smiling, our arms around each other's shoulders.

Five minutes later it was a great party. I'll never forget it as long as I live. People even brought me going away presents.

In fact, this diary I'm writing in was a present from Shelley. I don't know if she suspected what I'd use it for or not. Maybe she meant for me to keep track of my new life, whatever that turned out to be.

But when I unwrapped it, I knew it was just what I needed to fill the days until we left, to organize them and get my bearings. I knew I needed to write about leaving, about what that meant. My years here meant so much. They really, really did.

Do you understand?

10 *The Short but Wonderful New Life of Jack Shire's Pink Convertible*

I went home after the going away party and began packing up. It seemed like the right time to do it, as right as any time was likely to be. When I was pretty much finished, I went down to the kitchen where Mama and Daddy sat quietly together, drinking coffee.

"Okay, I'm ready now to hear where we're going," I said softly, pulling back a chair and sitting down. The kitchen looked strange, bare with all Mama's knickknacks boxed up and stored. Even the shade had been taken off the light, and the shadows were sharp and bare.

Mama looked across the table at Daddy nervously, and he looked down at his hands.

"Jenser, it looks like we'll be moving all the way to St. Louis. I could keep the job at Crestville, but we couldn't make ends meet on the minimum wage Mr. Douglas is able to pay me there. We need the prospects of a bigger place and we can stay with Aunt Clair and Uncle Bob in St. Louis until I find something so we can get a place of our own."

Daddy's voice was really funny. Something about it pushed me past the point where I was scared about going somewhere so big, to the point where I knew I'd better not be, for his sake and Mama's.

"When?" I asked.

"The auction is scheduled here for the third Saturday of July, Jens," Mama said, her voice tight. "We're going to try to be gone, out of the house, by then."

I nodded and stood up and went woodenly back to my room. I dug this diary out of the box of presents I'd brought back from the party and snuck back out to the hayloft to begin writing.

I've cried a lot the last few days while I've been trying to remember things the way they happened this spring and summer, but writing is a way of keeping your tears to yourself. Maybe I am growing up, at least a little. It seems important to me now not to make things harder on my parents than they already are.

I want to scream in these pages that this land is

ours, part of our very souls after so many generations. I want to yell and rant and rave. But none of that will help. None of it will stop the craving for the country hills and sunsets and smells and sounds. I miss them already, looking at them still. Everything bad happens a second at a time, and it helps to remember that. But there will come a second when we'll turn a corner and leave this behind forever. That's what seems impossible.

A funny thing happened last week, on the Fourth of July.

None of us felt much like celebrating, but we didn't think it was fair to Roger not to go into Iola to the fireworks that night. There was a parade too, down Main Street. Just a bunch of horses mostly, and a couple of new combines from the John Deere factory in Crestville. And, of course, the school band.

And then, bringing up the rear, who should appear but Jack Shire, driving the biggest and gaudiest of his six Oldsmobile convertibles. His red flannel shirt clashed happily with the bright pink of the car and he waved one arm all the time he was driving, sort of like you'd expect Miss America or somebody to do. The only difference was he occasionally leaned over the window to spit, a thing I'm sure Miss America is careful never to do.

"Well I'll be threashed if old Jack didn't get one

of those crazy cars to run," I heard my father say in an awed voice.

I looked up and down the street and saw the same awed expression on the faces of all the couple of hundred people watching Jack. The men were all shaking their heads, pushing the brims of their hats back and sticking their hands further into their overall pockets. Farmers do that when they are deeply, deeply impressed.

"Hi, Mr. Shire!" I yelled to him, waving for all I was worth, then clapping my hands. Roger clapped too, and together I thought we made a fairly decent cheering squad.

"Well, hello there, Jens Tucker!" Jack yelled back as he rolled slowly by. "Come on and hop in for a real parade ride, if you're a mind to!"

I thought Mama would put a hand on my shoulder to stop me, but I gave her a couple of seconds and when she didn't do it, I bolted into the street and around to the passenger side of the wonderful car.

"Just scramble right over, girl," Jack said, when he noticed I was struggling with the door handle. "I don't reckon that gadget has decided to work."

The car seemed huge from inside. The upholstery was lumpy and rich, the floor acres away from the panel. It was like riding in a floating palace of some kind, and I felt my face stretching into a wide grin.

"Go ahead, girlie! Wave to your public!" Jack told me, waving exuberantly still himself. So I did. I waved for all I was worth, as the band straggled around in front of us, playing something that I could tell was a song. I waved and waved as we rolled regally past the almost-crowd that was all the people in town.

"This is wonderful," I told Jack as we floated past Hempens Store, on toward the block with the church and gas station. "It's almost like magic."

"She's a beauty, all right," he said, laughing. "She's my ace in the hole, worth her weight in gold."

I wanted to ask how he had ever managed to get her running but I was afraid that might hurt his feelings.

Pretty soon, though, the parade ended. We ran out of street and rolled to a stop at the elevator. When Jack put his foot on the brake, the car made a clattering sound that seemed to me kind of final.

"Is it . . . dead?" I asked in a whisper.

"Oh, not dead so's you'd notice I don't believe," he said, patting the dashboard gently. "It may be I'll have to fetch Buddy Kinders to haul her with his truck and chain back to the garage, but she'll have her day again one of these times, I reckon."

I hated for the parade to be over. I hated to get out of the big magical car and go back to the problems of the real world. But I saw my family hurrying toward me and I knew the fireworks display would be starting before too long.

"Bye, Mr. Shire. And thanks," I told him. "I may not see you again. We're moving next week."

"So's I heard tell," he replied, pulling his pouch of chewing tobacco out of his shirt pocket. "Are you of a mind to leave?"

I looked down at my hands and shook my head.

"Well then, Miss Jens Tucker, I would like to offer you a piece of advice. Don't go."

I looked quickly up at him and smiled, thinking he was making some kind of joke. But he wasn't looking any less serious than usual.

"I have to," I said. "They're selling our house in two weeks."

"They're selling the buildings, but don't let anyone tell you to leave your home behind. You take it with you, here."

He was touching his chest, his heart. And I kind of knew then that was the main place he kept his convertibles—in his heart. That was probably why he could get them to run when everybody said it was hopeless. He mostly just sweet-talked them.

I nodded and shook the big red hand he held out.

"Thanks, Mr. Shire. See you."

Later, when we were settled on the curb of the sidewalk watching the fireworks bloom like flowers in the sky over the post office building, Buddy Kinders went by in his wrecker, and I knew he was heading over to take the sleeping pink mermaid back to her enchanted bank-building cave.

"You take a good bath when we get home, young lady," Mama told me. "It's hard telling what kind of wildlife has been sleeping in that awful car of Mr. Shire's."

It turns out that Brenda Miller is moving away next week too. She and her mother came over a couple of days after the Fourth of July to tell us good-bye. Mama and Brenda's mother sat in the kitchen, drinking coffee and crying a little, I think. Brenda and I sat in the living room, nibbling at the cookies Mama had brought in for us and feeling real funny and not knowing what to say. We've never been real close friends—just kind of friends since we're in the same class—and I've felt sort of funny around her ever since her father died. But now we were in the same boat, only she was going clear to California to live near her grandparents.

"Well, did you ever get a chance to use the chalk?" I asked finally, needing to say something.

"No, I really haven't felt like it." She looked sad still, and pale.

"Oh. Well, I hope you like it in California."

"Yeah, I hope so too. I hope you like St. Louis."

"Yeah."

She smiled and looked up for a second, then looked back down at the cookies. I wanted to say some things to her but I couldn't find the exact words.

"I had a rabbit but I let it go a few weeks ago," I finally said.

"Oh," she said. "By the way, I really liked the jelly beans."

"Really? I thought you probably hated them."

She looked up again and squinted her eyes. "Why would you think that, Jens?"

"I don't know," I said, clearing my throat first and crumbling up a cookie as I talked. "It was just kind of a stupid thing to give you, I guess. I mean, it was stupid to think we should give you all that stuff. I know more about things like that now. I mean, I know more how you felt. Still, we just wanted to do something, and that's all we could think of."

She nodded, her eyes bright. "Well, I ate the jelly beans, and my mother says sometime I'll feel like using the chalk, probably. I thought the whole thing was nice of you guys."

That was all we could think of to say. We just sat and ate and tried not to feel embarrassed. And then we could hear our mothers moving around in the kitchen and knew they were coming toward us.

"Jens?" Brenda whispered quickly, reaching out to touch my knee. "Listen. I have to tell you. Uh, just be glad you are all going together, you know?

Moving is hard, but it's not really the worst thing that could happen."

My stomach twisted into a tight knot for her when she said that, and I felt like crying. But I could only nod as our mothers came in, and Brenda got up, and pretty soon they left.

That night Daddy got home pretty early, while Roger was still up. After supper I sat for a long time on the stairs, watching Daddy and Mama together on the sofa, her head on his shoulder, Roger toddling around babbling to himself at their knees. And I knew our new house would still, somehow, be home.

11 *Good-bye*

Well, today is the day. Our last day here. Mama would kill me if she knew I was up so early. Or maybe she wouldn't. Maybe she'd understand why I needed to get up way before dawn. I'm starting to think we maybe are from the same planet after all, just from different parts of it or something.

I can't spend a long time writing today because I have to go through things one last time, beginning with seeing the morning star through the knothole in the milk barn. So when it gets light enough that I can turn off the flashlight and still see this page, I've got to finish up real quick and hide this journal in the hay and go down from the loft.

There isn't much left to say, anyhow. I should tell you so you won't worry that Betty and Petey are all right again, for the time being. Their mother came back, and Petey got out of the hospital, and they are all three living in their shacky little house in Iola. I saw Petey and Betty out begging yesterday when Mama and I went to put a change of address card in at the post office in Iola. Petey looked thinner and Betty was wearing my shoes.

Brenda moved two days ago, or so Mama told me. I haven't seen her since we had the cookies and couldn't think of what to say.

All kinds of people have been coming by our house this week, acting sad and even crying. It feels like someone's died, in a way. No, forget I wrote that. That was a childish thing to say. It would be much, much worse if someone had died.

I'm trying not to feel so sorry for myself, can you tell? I believe that's a sign of maturity.

Mr. Shire sent me a going away present, which I received in the mail yesterday. A photograph, taken with one of those cameras that spits the pictures right out, of the inside of his convertible garage.

Daddy couldn't figure it out. "Now why would that old Jack send you a picture of all this junk?" he asked me when I showed the picture to him.

Well, I couldn't, of course, admit to Daddy that I'd been inside the bank-turned-garage and had seen with my own eyes that it was magic in there. I wished I hadn't shown him the picture.

"I just got to be sort of friends with him," I said sheepishly, taking it quickly back. "You know, when I rode in the parade with him."

I turned the picture over, read the words again—

"Keep home inside of you, girlie. Don't leave till you're of a mind to, if'n you ever are."

I hope Betty and Petey make it. I hope Brenda and her mother have a good new life. I hope Mr. Jack Shire doesn't get laughed out of town, and is able to keep sweet-talking his convertibles into running occasionally.

I hope Arthur Boatright finds another girlfriend. Not that I was ever actually his girlfriend.

And I hope all kinds of stuff for my friends. We're getting together this afternoon at Marla's, just the four of us—Shelley, Kate, Marla, me. It'll be the three of them soon, but I'm not going to keep thinking and thinking about that.

"You could come back, you know," Marla said last week when we were riding bikes together. "In a few years when you're grown and on your own, I mean. You could move back here and get a job and buy back your farm."

I glanced over at her sparkling, hopeful eyes, and then looked across her shoulder at the wheat fields, turning amber. I had a lump in my throat that day, like I'll have for a while, I guess. There's just so much to say good-bye to, so many kinds of weather and fields and skies.

"Maybe," I shrugged, not wanting to talk a whole lot, "but I doubt it."

"Why?"

Poor Marla. She still thinks everything is fair in life, and easier than it is.

"I just don't imagine I could do something that my parents couldn't do, no matter how hard they tried, that's all. Now can we change the subject?"

"Well, still, anything's possible," she said.

It's getting a little bit light outside. Well, not light, but less dark. I've got to go. There are still a few pages in this diary I didn't get to fill. You can use them if you want.

Listen, if you find this and you're the new people, the people who bid the highest and got our land, I want you to know that I don't hold that against you. I'm not writing this to make you feel bad, or sad, or anything like that.

I'm writing this so you'll appreciate every minute and every second of what you've got.

I wish I could tell you how it felt to turn that last corner, the one that will seal our house from view. But I won't know that till tomorrow morning, when the moving van comes and Mama and Roger and I go on ahead in the car. I may not look back. I haven't decided for sure yet.

Anyway, I'm taking Mr. Shire's advice and carrying this place with me, hidden so deep inside that nothing can pull it out of my heart. I'll build on it. Everything I live from now on will sprout from it, like clover from seed.

There have been so many things to say good-bye to. And now, something inside me is about ready for some hellos.